Rich Girl

Berkley JAM titles by Carol Culver

The BFF Novels

MANDERLEY PREP

RICH GIRL

A BFF NOVEL

Rich Girl

CAROL CULVER

BERKLEY JAM, NEW YORK

THE BERKLEY PUBLISHING GROUP
Published by the Penguin Group
Penguin Group (USA) Inc.
375 Hudson Street, New York, New York 10014, USA
Penguin Group (Canada), 90 Eglinton Avenue East, Suite 700, Toronto, Ontario M4P 2Y3, Canada
(a division of Pearson Penguin Canada Inc.)
Penguin Books Ltd., 80 Strand, London WC2R 0RL, England
Penguin Group Ireland, 25 St. Stephen's Green, Dublin 2, Ireland (a division of Penguin Books Ltd.)
Penguin Group (Australia), 250 Camberwell Road, Camberwell, Victoria 3124, Australia
(a division of Pearson Australia Group Pty. Ltd.)
Penguin Books India Pvt. Ltd., 11 Community Centre, Panchsheel Park, New Delhi—110 017, India
Penguin Group (NZ), 67 Apollo Drive, Rosedale, North Shore 0632, New Zealand
(a division of Pearson New Zealand Ltd.)
Penguin Books (South Africa) (Pty.) Ltd., 24 Sturdee Avenue, Rosebank, Johannesburg 2196,
South Africa

Penguin Books Ltd., Registered Offices: 80 Strand, London WC2R 0RL, England

This book is an original publication of The Berkley Publishing Group.

PRINTING HISTORY
Berkley JAM trade paperback edition / January 2008

Library of Congress Cataloging-in-Publication Data

Culver, Carol, 1936–
Rich girl : a BFF novel / Carol Culver.—Berkley JAM trade pbk. ed.
p. cm.
Summary: Victoria's rich parents return to Hong Kong and leave her in their mansion with only a housekeeper, whose son attends exclusive Manderley Prep along with Victoria, and even though both students are interested in art, their differences seem far more glaring than anything they might share.
ISBN 978-0-425-21915-7 (trade pbk.)
[1. Interpersonal relations—Fiction. 2. Chinese Americans—Fiction. 3. Preparatory schools—Fiction. 4. High schools—Fiction. 5. Schools—Fiction:] I. Title.

PZ7.C906Ri 2008
[Fic]—dc22 2007034703

PRINTED IN THE UNITED STATES OF AMERICA

10 9 8 7 6 5 4 3 2 1

one

" 'It was the best of times, it was the worst of times.' "

Victoria Lee read the first sentence of *A Tale of Two Cities* over for the fourth time before it penetrated her tired brain. For her it *was* the best of times, considering her parents had finally left that morning. After spending two weeks with her at their suburban San Francisco McMansion, they were on their way back to Hong Kong.

On the other hand it was also the worst of times. Second semester of her junior year at Manderley Prep, the school where the progeny of Silicon Valley's movers and shakers went, *if* they could pass the stringent entrance exam or *if* their parents donated a new stadium or at least a new state-of-the-art theater. Her old friends were left far behind, she had a huge Dickens novel to read, and not much of a new social life in California.

Instead of reading any further, Victoria got out her case of cedarwood colored pencils and sketched the outline of a dress on a blank page in her notebook. In less than a minute she was more engrossed in getting the lines of the slouchy sweater dress right than she could ever be in any old nineteenth century novel. Now if that novel had pictures of nineteenth century fashions, that would be another matter.

"Homework already? The semester hasn't even started."

It was Cindy, her best friend at Manderley—her only friend really—who'd joined her on the second floor of the T. J. Ransom Memorial Library.

Victoria shoved her notebook aside. "Just fooling around, wasting time." That's what her parents would say. *Wasting time drawing clothes. Fashion design? Just what the world needs, another designer making clothes no real woman in her right mind would wear.* That was the point. She would design clothes for real women.

"Good vacation?" Cindy asked, setting her backpack on the corner table.

Victoria sighed. "What vacation? My parents came to town

and I never had a chance to catch my breath. When I wasn't chauffeuring them to business meetings in Silicon Valley, they were dragging me to the art museums in San Francisco."

"I thought you liked art."

"Not the kind they like. They love the Palace of the Legion of Honor with all those old European pictures. Portraits of fat rich women stuffed into satin dresses and the stiffs they married standing next to them. I wanted to go to the MOMA with the cool abstract paintings. But no. Next it was, what else? The Asian Art Museum. As if they couldn't get their fill of Asian art in Hong Kong. I went to a coffee shop and tried to read my book there while they insisted I was denying my heritage. What heritage? I said, 'I've got two.' In case they forgot. Of course we had to stop in Chinatown for a tour of a fortune cookie factory."

"You can't get fortune cookies in Hong Kong?"

"Would you believe fortune cookies are a San Francisco invention?"

"Like Rice-A-Roni?"

"I guess so." Victoria reached into the Vuitton Murakami bag she got for Christmas the year before, pulled out a cellophane-wrapped fortune cookie and handed it to Cindy. "We came back with a half-gallon carton of cookies. This one's for you. You'll see why. Go ahead, open it."

"Mmmm, this looks good. They make chocolate-dipped fortune cookies?"

"Chocolate, coconut, strawberry, traditional, jumbo and everything in between. You name it, they make it. We saw the whole thing because the owners are friends of my parents. The assembly line, the chocolate vats, everything. They do special fortunes for showers, parties, weddings or whatever, with fortunes like, 'He loves me, he loves me not. He loves me, we tied the knot.' "

Victoria wrinkled her nose at this sappy verse. If she ever got married, she'd avoid both the sticky sentiment and the cookie factory.

Cindy opened her cookie and read the fortune. " 'You will get 2400 on your SATs and travel across a great ocean.' " Her face lit up. "Hey, do these come true?"

"Guaranteed or your money back," Victoria said. "I thought you'd like that."

"What's in your future this semester?" Cindy asked as she bit into her cookie.

"Right now all I want is a nap. I dropped my parents at the airport this morning at six. I'm so tired I can barely keep my eyes open. Especially when I'm trying to read *A Tale of Two Cities* for Brit Lit." Victoria held up her book. "It's got about a thousand pages."

"But don't you see?" Cindy said eagerly, brushing the cookie crumbs off her sweater. "This could be your story. Your life. A tale of two cities. Your mom's city, Hong Kong, and your dad's city, San Francisco."

Victoria thumbed through the book. "Is that what it's about?" she asked hopefully. Cindy would know. She was so smart. And the best part was she didn't act like she knew everything. Rare for Manderley.

"Not really. Those cities are London and Paris, and the year is 1775, but it's really a good book once you get into it."

"I can't get into it. I've tried, and look, I'm still on page one. Honestly they should sell it as an alternative to Ambien. Non-habit-forming and guaranteed to work. Every time I pick it up I feel my eyes getting heavy. I need help, like SparkNotes or watching the movie. Something." If only she could study with Steve, who she knew was going to be in her class this semester. Not that he was so smart, but it would give her an excuse to get together with him.

"I can help you. I read it last year. Hey, you look great," Cindy said, leaning back in her chair. "Cute jumper. So you had time for some shopping over the vacation."

Victoria blushed, happy that someone noticed. She should be satisfied knowing she felt good in what she wore, but having somebody like Cindy notice, someone who didn't normally pay attention to her clothes or anyone else's, was especially sweet. "I made it. Not the shoes though or the leggings."

"Really? I can't believe it. Your parents must be so proud of you."

"Not exactly. They think sewing is a giant time-sucker. In Hong Kong you can have a tailor make you a suit for fifty dollars. Not to mention all the stores there. They always remind me I can hop on a ferry for Tsim Sha Tsui and shop for bargains at the I.T. Sale Shop. They don't see why I should bother making my own clothes."

"Why do you?"

"Everything in the stores is trendy and disposable. Or it doesn't fit. I know what I want but nobody's designed it yet. Besides, I love the whole process, from drawing the pattern to cutting the fabric and then fitting and wearing it. There's nothing like that feeling of doing it all myself."

"You're amazing. Nobody else I know makes her own clothes and lives on her own too. Your parents must really trust you. A lot of kids would go wild and have parties nonstop if they didn't have their parents around breathing down their necks."

"I'd like to have a party but I don't have any friends to invite. The reason my parents left me here is all about the business," Victoria explained. "They bought the house so they could have a residence here. Someone has to live in it and that's me. As a bonus I get to go to Manderley which should get me into UC Berkeley." Victoria's weak smile turned into a frown. "At least that's the plan." She didn't say that it wasn't *her* plan.

Living alone certainly had its advantages. No parents around telling her what to do. A feeling of freedom that was sometimes scary but mostly exhilarating. Of course they e-mailed her all the time, but that was different. When she first came to California, Victoria had been so homesick without her best friends she begged her parents to let her come back. Of course they said no. Cindy had helped her get over it just by being her first Manderley friend.

"Actually, when my parents were here they hired a house-keeper and now she lives in the apartment above the garage. She's supposed to keep the house clean, do the laundry and oversee the grounds."

"What about you, is she supposed to oversee you too?"

"If she tries, I'll have to set her straight. I've gotten used to my independence and in the past two weeks I've had enough advice and orders to last me years. I tell you it was a shock after being on my own."

"Did you see Steve over the break?"

Victoria shook her head. She'd really missed him. If you can miss someone you hardly ever saw but really, really liked.

Steve Heller was the ultimate all-American boy. Blond, blue-eyed, buff and gorgeous. *And* he was studying Chinese. *And* his father was a well-known lawyer in Silicon Valley who made lucrative deals with China for his clients. *And* last but definitely not least, Steve was the star of the basketball team. Victoria hadn't missed a single game.

He wasn't exactly her boyfriend the way Marco was Cindy's, but she thought he liked her. She knew she liked him. Who wouldn't? He was the epitome of the uber California guy. Cindy said they made a great-looking couple. He didn't have another girlfriend, from what she knew. Maybe when basketball season was over he'd have time for a girlfriend. She just hoped it would be her.

"I thought about calling him," Victoria said.

"Didn't you read that book about how to tell if he's not that into you?"

"If it's not on the required reading list, I haven't read it."

"It should be. Here's how it goes: If you haven't heard from him, he's just not that into you."

"What if he's too busy to call me?"

"Those who know say there's no such thing. When men want you, even if they've got homework, college counseling, SAT prep, football practice, yoga, or Tae Kwon Do, they'll find time to make their move, and they do the work."

"I guess maybe he just wants to be friends," Victoria said with a sigh.

"He took you to the Welcome Dance, didn't he?"

"But that was our one and only date. Anyway, he's been away so I didn't expect to hear from him. He told me he was going skiing in Tahoe with his family for the whole vacation," Victoria said. "Maybe there's no cell phone service in the mountains."

"Hmm, maybe. I thought . . . no, I guess not."

"What?"

"I thought I saw his mother come in to the spa last week for a facial when I was working. Maybe she got tired of schussing down the slopes and needed to get rid of her sun spots. Anyway, are you going to be Steve's tutor again this semester?"

"I hope so. I don't know if he'll still need me. He may drop Chinese this semester."

"That doesn't mean he'll drop you. If he likes you he'll think of a way to see you."

"We're going to be in the same English class this semester so I'm bound to run into him, but I can't be his English tutor. Not if I can't read the book."

"There are other subjects you could tutor him in, if you know what I mean," Cindy said with a gentle nudge.

Victoria dropped her pencil and shot a quizzical glance at

her friend. "You don't mean sex, do you?" She glanced over her shoulder to make sure they were alone in that part of the library. Just the subject she was dying to broach but was afraid to bring up herself. "If anyone needs lessons in sex ed, which we didn't have at my school, it's me. And soon. I've been very protected."

"Wait, you were Miss Junior Hong Kong. You must have had guys falling all over you so you could have your pick."

"Yes, but they were all either dorky or too smooth. Besides, my mother was always watching me like a peregrine falcon."

"Isn't that an endangered species?"

"So's my mother. She went after her prey, my father, like a falcon, and she caught him. Not that he resisted. He thinks he got the best of that deal. A beauty queen with smarts and a great life in Hong Kong where he gets to improve his Chinese every day. His Chinese is now better than my mother's. Anyway, she was my chaperone during my reign. Her plan is for me to marry well like she did. Well means smart and rich, of course. And to remain a virgin until my wedding night like she did. She made me practice looking down my nose at guys who would come on to me. She told me to act like I had an invisible shield around me. Like I'm too good for them. Honestly, it was like *The Princess Diaries*. My mom is a Chinese version of Julie Andrews. I told her I couldn't promise anything."

"How did she take it?"

"What can she do? She's a zillion miles away. She can't wait up for me, screen my dates if I had any, or do any matchmaking. Besides, she's the last person I'd ask for advice about anything sexual. Even kissing would be too dirty a topic for her."

"Really? Even just how to kiss? The whole 'close eyes, open lips, tilt head, run tongue over lips, kiss cheeks, trail your lips to his lips, open mouth but no tongue at first, make sure arms around partner' thing?"

"Oh, no, I mean well, yes, that kind of thing." Victoria felt silly sucking up the basics like a sponge, but how else was she going to learn? Anyway, this was Cindy. She wouldn't laugh at her for being hopelessly naïve.

"Well, my mom isn't here, so I can finally do what all the other girls are doing." As soon as she found out what that was. "She'll never know. She's got the family business to run while my dad writes up a new economic plan for Hong Kong. See what I've got to live up to?"

"You're lucky to have parents who care what you do. Irina, my stepmom, cares that I'm around to be her slave, to help her run the spa, and that's about it."

"That sucks," Victoria said sympathetically.

"It's okay, I'm used to it," Cindy said brightly.

Victoria didn't know how Cindy coped with her nasty stepmother and those two vicious stepsisters who'd done their best to ruin Cindy's romance with Marco. She had guts, and so much determination to get what she wanted, Victoria was determined not to complain about her own situation ever again. At least not in front of Cindy.

She glanced out the floor-to-ceiling window to see that students were straggling in, sluggish after two weeks off. She searched the crowd for a tall blond boy but she didn't see him. Not the one she was looking for anyway.

She'd been counting the days until school started and it wasn't because she missed the academic challenge. Far from it. At least she'd see him last period in English. Unless he'd changed his schedule.

What would she say when she saw him? *How did you like the book? Did you have a good time skiing? Do you have a girlfriend I don't know about? It can't be that you're too busy or intimidated to ask me out, so what is it? Are you . . . just not that into me?*

She had to stop thinking about Steve so much. She not only needed lessons in kissing, she needed basic flirting skills. How do you make it clear you're interested in someone without scaring them off? Was it true that when men want you, they'll find a way? How do you know if someone only likes you because you're rich and you were once a beauty queen? Fortunately here at Manderley almost everyone was rich and no one but Cindy knew she was Miss Junior Hong Kong. She turned back to her friend.

"So did you see Marco over the holidays?"

"He went back to Italy to have Christmas with his family, but he sent me this postcard." Cindy pulled out a hand-painted card with a photograph of houses spilling down the cliff toward the azure sea.

"Ohhh, is this where he lives?" Victoria turned the card over and saw the message was in Italian. "What does he say?" she asked.

Cindy grinned. "Oh, just the usual. You know how Italians are."

"I don't think I do."

"They're very, uh, out there. I had to look up most of the words in my dictionary. I'm not sure whether my Italian is up to it."

"There's no question he's definitely into you," Victoria said. "If I met someone who looked like a Greek god and played soccer like a pro and wrote romantic postcards and who'd invited me to visit him in Italy next summer, I'd be willing to lose my virginity. I mean, what's it good for anyway?"

Victoria really wished someone would tell her. She was pretty sure she and Cindy were both still virgins. What were they waiting for? What would it take?

"Good question, Victoria."

That wasn't the answer Victoria was looking for. That wasn't an answer at all. She wanted to know if Cindy was having sex with Marco and should she, Victoria, offer herself to Steve. And if so, how?

Instead she rephrased the question. "What I want to know is do all American high school girls have sex? Does it matter who with? Or is it just important to do it by a certain age?"

"Yes, no, and yes," Cindy said.

"Well that's more than I learned at my last school. Of course it was an all-girls school so we were all in the dark."

"A girls school? I wouldn't like that," Cindy said.

"It's different. No one dresses up. We wore uniforms. No makeup. Why bother? For fun we'd get together on the weekends to have facials. Then I did everyone's hair for them. I'm pretty good at it actually." Victoria studied Cindy's deep red curly hair.

"Has anyone ever told you you have gorgeous hair?" Victoria asked.

"A few people," she said.

It was no surprise Cindy didn't realize how stunning her hair was or could be. Some days it looked like Cindy had barely combed it. If Victoria had hair that color she'd be wearing clothes in vivid colors. She'd wear her hair smooth and shiny, and that's not all she'd do.

"You could use a good shaping," Victoria said gently so as not to hurt Cindy's feelings. "Why don't you let me cut it for you?"

Cindy self-consciously ran her hand through her hair. "Really? You wouldn't mind?"

"Are you kidding? I live for that kind of stuff—hair, clothes, jewelry, makeup."

"I don't wear makeup."

Victoria sighed. "I know, but you should. Just a touch. I can show you."

Then she leaned back in her chair. She was exhausted. She'd been up for hours. Now she had to go to math class when she'd much rather do a makeover for her friend. Her parents insisted she take advanced algebra even though she was terrible at math. Their plan was for her to get an MBA at Harvard, then after marrying some suitably ambitious man, come back to Hong Kong to participate in the family business. Victoria had other plans.

two

You have more questions than answers; deal with it.

—Golden Gate Fortune Cookies
(Fast, Fresh and Flavorable)

Gabe Thomas's life had changed radically in the past two weeks. Last semester he'd been suspended for a week from Castle High School for covering a wall with graffiti and some other harmless stuff. At Castle the emphasis was on football, which he didn't play, but the most popular sport was making fun of the rich kids across town at Manderley Prep. Now he was one of them. Not rich, but one them anyway. How it had happened so fast, he didn't understand. Didn't they know about his past? Didn't they care that he was a troublemaker? Where was the money for his tuition coming from?

"I lost my job," his mom had said one day last month when

he came home from school. They were living in a cottage on the grounds of a big estate in Bellview, where his mother was the housekeeper and nanny. He stopped in the middle of the room and dropped his backpack. "The Hendersons are moving to New York," she explained.

"Didn't they want you to go with them?" They always said they couldn't get along without her. They loaded her down with gifts and perks like a health club membership and the lease of a new car, terrified some other family would lure her away with a higher salary. Now what were they going to do?

"Yes, but I said no. California is our home. Don't worry, I'll find another job around here."

Sure enough, before he knew it, she had another job and suddenly they were living in an apartment above the garage on an estate owned by some rich Chinese people who didn't even live there. Go figure. Some people had more money than they knew what to do with.

Instead of regretting losing the Hendersons, his mom decided change was a good thing. Not just a new job for her, but a new school for Gabe. And some new friends. She didn't like the bad crowd he hung out with on the beach at night, who smoked pot and drank beer. She was more angry at him for getting in trouble at school. Jeez, talk about an overreaction. It was only a one-week suspension. This wasn't ordinary graffiti, this was his own graphic impression of global warming—in other words, a political statement. But nobody at Castle appreciated it. They might have if they'd had time, but he'd been forced to wash it off the next day as part of his punishment.

Then he had to quit his job at Starbucks because his mom said he wouldn't have time with all the homework at Manderley. When he complained about spending money she said she'd pay him to haul out the garbage at the new house.

The next thing he knew he was standing in line in front of Manderley Hall to register for classes where he didn't know a single person. Even if his mom had talked them into taking him at Manderley, he didn't know how she got the twenty-eight thousand a year it took for him to go there. Did she hit up his dad for the money? That would be a first. His dad had been MIA since he was born.

How did she get this new job so fast anyway? Sure, she was good at what she did. So good the family begged her to go with them. They said they couldn't get along without her running their house. She said no one is indispensable. So they swallowed their disappointment and wrote her a glowing letter of recommendation. In a matter of days she had this new job and he was at a new school, far away from his old crowd. From the looks of the kids here, the cars they drove and the clothes they wore, he was probably the only one whose mother was a housekeeper.

When he complained about leaving Castle, she had said, "If you liked it so much, why did you spray paint the wall?"

"Just expressing myself," he muttered. "Making a statement. You wouldn't understand."

Next she'd made him take the entrance test and then had gone to see the admissions director at Manderley. When she got back she looked pleased. Pleased and determined.

"You got into the best prep school in the state," she said. "You're smart and you're lucky. If you don't want to end up doing housework for rich people, don't screw it up. And if you want to express yourself and make a statement, do it on paper. I'll frame it and hang it on the wall." When she talked like that, it was pointless to argue.

"I thought you liked your job," he said, watching her peel apples in the large kitchen of their new apartment. Even though it was just the two of them and no big family in residence, she'd rolled out the crust for two pies. He looked out the window at the orchard, the pool house, the hedges, and the carefully kept grounds that surrounded the huge main house with its ostentatious turrets and gables. Did she ever wish for a house like that instead of the servant quarters, however nice they might be? Was that what this was about? Turning him into the person she wanted to be?

All he knew was she couldn't stand to see apples on a tree

going to waste. Couldn't stand to see him wasting time either. Or wasting his so-called talent drawing on walls.

Never catch her wasting time. She never stopped working. Never stopped managing. Never stopped thinking. She's the one who should have gone to Manderley. Instead, maybe she was going to go there vicariously.

"I do like my job," she said. "For now. Money's good. The boss halfway around the world. Hours can't be beat. But I want something else for you. You better want it too."

"Sure, Ma," he said.

"Don't humor me," she said, snapping a dish towel in his direction.

He grinned. No use trying to bullshit his mom. She saw right through him. Maybe because she was young enough to be his older sister. Sometimes she acted like one. And now was not the time to tell her he didn't want to go to school with a bunch of rich snobs. Now was the time to keep his mouth shut and do what she said and paint something for her just to see if she'd really hang it on the wall. Later she'd realize what he already knew—he was a misfit wherever he was and this rich kid school wasn't the right place for him either.

"Does my dad know?"

She dropped her apple peeler. "Know what?"

"About Manderley. Did he go there too? Is that why I'm going? Is he paying for it?"

She glared at him. He'd broken her Rule Number One. He'd asked a question with the word dad in it.

"Gabe," she said sharply.

He got the message. We Don't Talk About Him.

three

Some give up the pursuit of happiness for the happiness of pursuit.

—Golden Gate Fortune Cookies
(For all your cookie needs)

Gabe's mom had never approved of the kids he hung out with at Castle. She thought they were a bad influence on him. Looking around on his first day at Manderley, he didn't see any big improvement in the quality of the kids there except for their high-priced designer jeans and their expensive cars. If that was your definition of "quality."

Oh, yeah, there was that exotic looking girl in his art class. There was no one with that kind of quality at Castle. Almond-shaped eyes, shiny black hair that brushed her high cheekbones. She was dressed like an upscale fashion model. Maybe she was. He hadn't seen any girl that out-and-out beautiful anywhere except in magazines. More than beautiful, she had a look about her that said she was a cut above everyone else. Especially him. Which didn't stop him from lusting after her of course.

He kept sneaking glances in her direction, trying to figure her out. New like him? Or had she been there since middle school? That would explain her cool, I-know-my-way-around-here-and-you-don't attitude. Was she smart, dumb, rich? What else?

Disappointment Number One: When he sat down next to her, shoved the hair out of his eyes for a closer look and said, "Hi," she looked down her patrician nose at him. Okay, he got the message. If he had been back at Castle he'd know how to act—with some hefty attitude and a few snarky, underhanded comments just to see how thick that perfect skin really was. But he wasn't there, he was here, so he kept his attitude to himself and his mouth shut.

Here he wasn't important enough for her to bother with. She probably knew instinctively that his father wasn't the CEO of some Fortune 500 company. Shit, even he didn't know who his father was. Maybe he had dropped out of Harvard to start a multimillion-dollar company like Bill Gates had done. Maybe he started his own software business in a garage like Hewlett and Packard. Maybe he *was* a CEO. Or a famous athlete. Naaah, if he was, Gabe would be good at a sport, any sport. He wasn't.

Disappointment Number Two: The model in their life drawing class was not nude. She was wearing a bathing suit. Not even a bikini. It didn't matter. He wasn't there to draw female figures. Or lose his head over some girl who thought she was too good for him. He was there to use class time for his own purposes. He'd always gotten away with it at Castle.

The art teacher, a tall guy named Julian who had a flowing mane of hair, a nose like a beak and a generic European accent, made the rounds, looking over students' shoulders and making comments.

He held up a sketch in front of the class and said, "What stands out when you look at this picture?"

"The face," Gabe said. "I mean, it's not there."

"Is the face important? No, it isn't," Julian said. "It's all about the body. Isn't it obvious?"

Gabe shrugged. No, it wasn't obvious. Not to him.

"What does this tell you about the artist?" Julian asked the class.

"He's good at following directions," the cool girl next to him said. "But that's all." It sure didn't sound like a compliment.

Julian nodded and walked over to see what she was drawing.

"What's that?" the teacher asked her.

Out of the corner of his eye, he could see her blush. So she wasn't made of ice after all. Julian held up her sketch. It was a picture of a tall model, her face turned at a haughty angle, wearing high-heeled shoes, a ruffled shirt and wide-cuffed pants. She looked nothing like the model in their class.

"Someone thinks this is a class in commercial art," Julian said. "It isn't. This is life drawing. We're drawing bodies here. Bodies without clothes. If that's a problem for you . . ."

She didn't say anything. Gabe saw her temple throb and he wondered if she was the kind of girl who burst into tears at the slightest criticism. Apparently not. She'd quickly pulled herself together and she was giving Julian her best superior look as if to say *who the hell are you* and *where do* you *get off criticizing* my *work?*

"For your information this is *my* art class. We're here to express ourselves. Within limits. In case anyone else is thinking of drawing whatever they want instead of the assignment, it's not too late to drop this class."

Gabe grabbed his drawing and crumpled it up in his fist. Why wait until Julian dissed his sketch too and encouraged him to drop?

"Not so fast," Julian said, his arm reaching out to stop Gabe from tossing his sketch in the wastebasket. "You're Gabe Thomas, aren't you? I heard about you. You like to draw, huh? Let's see what you've got there." He smoothed the paper and held it up to the class, wrinkles and all. Gabe squirmed in his seat.

"Interesting," Julian said. "Another person who can't follow directions. What is this? I know it's not the model here. Clouds, water, guns and steel. Does this look like the model to you?" he asked the class.

Gabe clenched his teeth together to keep from blurting out something he'd be sorry for. Who would have thought an art teacher would be such a tightass? What a way to start off his career at Manderley.

four

This will be a memorable time in your life, no matter how hard you try to forget it.

—Golden Gate Fortune Cookies
(Excellent products, worry-free orders)

"Victoria Lee? I'm Brooke Nelson, your big sister."

It was one hour later and Victoria was standing at her locker, still shaking all over from that scene in art class where the teacher made a fool of her in front of everyone.

Her big sister? She was big all right, tall and blonde and busty, the kind of sexy body type guys found irresistible. She was wearing straight-leg black jeans, a big white men's shirt knotted at the waist with a black tank top under it, and Uggs. Victoria admired a daring sense of fashion, but Brooke was making too much of a mixed statement. In her mind she re-dressed Brooke in a miniskirt and a vest and redid her eyes with dark eye shadow for a smoky look. Only in her mind, of course, because whatever else she wore, Brooke sported a layer of self-assurance Victoria was learning to accept as normal at Manderley. Imagine what she would say if Victoria told her that her clothes were all wrong for her. *"Excuuuuse me?"* she'd ask with disbelief.

"My what?" Victoria said.

"You're new, right?" Brooke said.

"I was new in the fall, but . . ."

"Sorry I didn't get around to looking you up till now. I've been *so* busy. First the fall cotillion. What a scene that was—the white dress, the Ritz-Carlton, the first dance with Daddy, you know the drill."

"Uh-huh." Victoria knew the drill. A bunch of bland blonde debutantes all dressed alike in boring strapless white dresses. If she were a deb she'd design her own dress, something cutting edge, and shock them all. But she wasn't. Her mother had wanted her to do it, but she'd refused.

One of the few times she'd actually overruled her mother. She suspected all the debutantes were like Brooke, and she wanted no part of the whole phony scene. Naturally she didn't voice this opinion. After all, she'd been wanting to meet more people, maybe she ought to give Brooke a break. But after a seemingly endless two-minute break where Brooke had continued to babble, she was done cutting her "sister" slack of any kind.

"Then for Christmas vacation we were at Sun Valley."

"How nice," Victoria murmured. Actually, her parents were thinking of buying a condo there. But if the place was filled with people like Brooke . . .

"It's okay, really," Victoria assured her. "I can see you're way too busy to be a big sister. Besides, I really don't need one."

"Doesn't matter. You've got me. It's part of community service. You have to put in so many hours. Otherwise I'd have to go to Mexico and dig latrines for poor people." She shuddered. "Or join Habitat for Humanity and build houses in some dismal neighborhood right in this country. Ugh. Instead I'm going to help you through your first year at Manderley." She gave Victoria an unmistakably patronizing smile.

"Actually, there is something you can help me with. I signed up for chemistry, but I want to get out of it."

Brooke shook her head. "As your big sis, I have to tell you, Victoria, that dropping chemistry is not such a hot idea. Chemistry is going to look really good on your transcript."

"Not if I get a D."

"You're not going to get a D because what you do when you get to class is pick a smart partner, a guy who'll do the experiments for you and write them up. That way you'll get whatever grade he gets and you'll get the credit, know what I mean?"

"How do I know who's smart and who's not?" Victoria asked, playing along with this obnoxious girl who was determined to run her life. She'd just gotten rid of her parents and now this.

"Easy. They'll have glasses, a laptop in a briefcase and a pocket full of pens and stuff. Plus they'll look like geeks. You do know what geeks look like, don't you? Do I have to draw you a picture?"

Victoria shook her head. Obviously Brooke was into playing the smart-ass big sister, but why did she have to be *her* smart-ass big sister?

"So I don't drop chemistry, but what if I drop life drawing?" Victoria asked.

"Life drawing as in art? You want to drop art?" Brooke looked at her like she was demented. "Come on, that has got to be one easy A. Nope, my advice is to relax and draw pictures. I gotta run now, Vicky," she said. "If you have any more questions like who's who and who isn't who, give me a call. It's easy to make a mistake when you're new, and you so don't want to end up hanging out with the wrong people."

Victoria cringed. First, nobody called her Vicky. Second, life drawing was not going to be an easy A, and no smart geek partner was going to do her work for her, no matter how hard chemistry was. And another thing, Victoria would hang out with whoever she wanted whether they were the "right" people or not. But Brooke was gone and Victoria knew it was pointless trying to tell seniors anything because they were sure they knew everything, especially Brooke.

five

Commit yourself to the dark forces or you'll never get what you want.

—Golden Gate Fortune Cookies
(The cookie with the personalized message inside)

The chemistry lab smelled like rotten eggs. Maggie Stewart didn't want to be there. She hated the smell and she hated science. Then she saw Ethan across the room and she changed her mind. Maybe signing up for chemistry wasn't such a bad idea after all.

She would have smiled at him but since she still had braces (the only high school junior *still* wearing braces) she kept her mouth shut and waved instead.

He wouldn't ask her to be his partner, after all, they barely exchanged greetings these days and she sure wasn't going to ask him. Ever since she'd moved out of their upscale neighborhood to a suburb where some people were so poor they didn't even have a gardener they didn't seem to have much to say to one another. All she needed was a rejection to start the spring semester off with a bang.

If she was going to ask anybody it would be that girl Victoria who also seemed to be alone.

"Um, do you have a partner?" Maggie asked her.

"Uh, no, but . . ."

Oh shit. She didn't want her either. "It's okay, you're waiting for someone."

"It's not that. I don't know anyone really. The thing is, I'm terrible at science. For sure you don't want to be my partner."

Just then the teacher, Mr. Kashigian, came into the room wearing a red T-shirt with "Science is Fun" in white letters. The problem was solved when the first thing he did was assign partners. Maggie felt a rush of disappointment when she got a tall skinny guy with curly hair who looked like Napoleon Dynamite. Not that she'd expected to get Ethan, but a girl can always dream. While she was dreaming she might as well dream about ditching her glasses and getting contact lenses too.

She'd seen her partner around campus playing chess on the lawn at lunchtime. That's the kind of guy he was. The kind who'd probably be good at chemistry at least.

Maggie looked over at Victoria at the next table. Her

partner was a cute but scruffy *American Idol* look-alike with hair hanging in his face. But Victoria didn't look happy either. In fact, she caught Maggie's gaze and rolled her eyes. Some people didn't know when they had it good. Who knows? Maybe she'd landed a partner who'd sing romantic songs like that guy who'd almost won on *Idol. And* be good at chemistry.

Out of the corner of her eye Maggie noticed Ethan was paired with a blond cheerleader, at least she used to be a cheerleader before the sport was banned last semester for indecent exposure and improper behavior on and off the field.

The second thing Mr. Kashigian did after assigning partners was to prove that "science was fun" by boiling red cabbage on his Bunsen burner and filling the whole room with steam and the smell of cabbage. Some of the girls made gagging noises and held their noses. Then he measured the pH of the water left in his pot. Maggie couldn't concentrate. She kept looking across the room to where Ethan and the former cheerleader had their heads together. She felt a pain in her chest. That could have been her with him. It should have been her. If only life was fair and turned out the way you wanted it to. It was hard to pay attention to the experiment under those conditions.

Contrary to what the teacher said, chemistry was not only

not fun, it was useless. Sure, you could test the pH of your cabbage or your swimming pool water. What good would that do Maggie? The house with the pool went up for sale after the divorce.

Mr. K (as he wanted to be called) announced the chemical of the week—arsenic. He passed out periodic tables, a class calendar and some other lists and schedules. Then he made the students write down the cardinal rule of chemistry: To prove your results, your experiment has to be repeatable under different conditions.

"In case anyone's afraid of chemistry, I'm going to prove to you that science is fun! No, it's not all bangs and flashes and explosions. Sometimes it's just atoms bonding. That can be fun too. For homework you can choose any one of the simple home experiments on the handout and report back tomorrow on your results. The choice is yours, folks, floating soap bubbles, the fireproof balloon, the collapsing can . . ."

Sarcastic comments were flying all over the classroom.

"Wow, soap bubbles. I've never had so much fun."

"I'll tell you what's fun, blowing up the lab."

"Watch out. Mr. K's gonna explode and all that bullshit will splatter all over the lab."

"Fathead's coming this way."

Maggie frowned. Mr. K might be a dork. What teacher

wasn't? At least he was nice about it. What was the point of laughing at him?

Mr. K went on and on, oblivious to the babble of snarky comments. Maggie agreed that science could be fun. With the right partner. High school could be fun too. With the right partner.

six

Read books, it will take your mind off yourself.

—Golden Gate Fortune Cookies
(Cookies your guests will never forget)

Yes, it was a small school, but still, what were the chances of Victoria having the same guy in two of her classes? And if it was going to happen, why couldn't it be Steve? No, it was this rebel with the hair in his face who didn't follow directions. Okay, she didn't follow directions either, but at least she'd drawn something recognizable.

She and whoever he was didn't exchange a single word during the whole chemistry class. What was there to say to someone who sat there taking notes about measuring the acid in rainwater like it was the most fascinating thing he'd ever done. Not only that, as soon as class was over, he went up to talk to the teacher.

Only the truly nerdy did that. He didn't look like a classic case from Brooke's description, but you couldn't always tell.

Now with Steve there was no doubt at all. No one could be less like a nerd. No pencils in his front pocket, no calculator, no computer. Just pure muscle and bone wrapped in a faded T-shirt with UCLA stretched across it, ripped jeans and flip-flops. He was late to English class so she hadn't been able to talk to him. She could only sneak glances across the classroom to see that he hadn't gotten any uglier during the vacation. In fact, he'd gotten a gorgeous tan, probably on the slopes.

No wonder she didn't catch much of the discussion of *A Tale of Two Cities*. She was too busy drooling over him and planning what she'd say to him after class.

How was your vacation? No, too ordinary.

How was Tahoe? Where would that lead? He'd just say, "Great," and the conversation would be over.

Want to get together and study? Why would he want to study with someone who hadn't read the book yet?

She had to think of a conversation starter that would lead to something, like renting the movie—provided they'd made a movie of such a boring book.

It came as no surprise when she didn't know what to say when Ms. Oggle, the oldest living teacher at Manderley, asked Victoria to name some of the many themes in the book.

How could Victoria think about themes when she kept wondering why anyone would put up with wrinkles in this day and age? Had the woman never heard of Botox? Then there was her hair. No one let their hair go gray anymore. What about contact lenses? They weren't that expensive. Even on a teacher's salary she could spring for them. Sure, she was old, but come on, did she have to *look* so old? How did the woman expect anyone to concentrate on literature when her appearance shouted out, *Help me! I'm old and I just don't care.* Victoria would never be that old.

She frantically leafed through the pages of the paperback book hoping something would leap out at her, but it didn't. The harder Victoria tried to think, the more she felt braindead. The silence in the room was deafening. All she could hear was her heart pounding in her ears while she felt the blood rushing to her head.

Finally someone in the front row, where only the true dorks sat, volunteered his thoughts, which Victoria scribbled down like mad. *Dramatic contrasts. Caught in Rev. Rumours.* No, *rumors.* She had to drop the British spelling. She was in America now. *Guilt, shame,* she wrote. *Death of old leads to new.*

Then it was on to the possible topics for the paper. A paper. No one had told her about a paper. As if she didn't have enough to do. Hopefully one of these topics wouldn't be so hard; *Re-*

demption. Patriotism. Transformation. But they all sounded so abstract. She hated abstract, except in art. What that weirdo in her class was attempting to draw.

Even after listening to Ms. Oggle rattle on and on, she still couldn't imagine writing a ten-page paper on any one of the topics. Tomorrow she'd plan to focus on the discussion instead of her teacher's lack of style or one impossibly hot guy who sat across the room looking out the window instead of at her.

As soon as class was over Victoria ignored the advice Cindy had imparted and jumped out of her seat to try to catch Steve, but he was faster than she was. He probably had some kind of practice. Victoria didn't even know what sport he'd be playing this semester.

She sighed. One day down. One hundred something left. Time to face the facts. He just wasn't that into her.

"Can I give you a ride someplace?" Victoria asked Maggie when she saw her in the parking lot.

"I have to go to work." Maggie looked at her watch. "At the mall."

"You work at the mall? I'd love to work there. Then I'd get a discount on clothes. But I don't dare get a job. My parents think I should spend every minute studying and getting good grades. Where do you work, Forever 21?" That would be so cool. It would also be cool to work on Maggie too. Victoria's fingers itched to highlight her hair, wax her eyebrows, get rid of her braces and get her some new clothes. Nothing flashy. Just something that brought out the best in her. That was the challenge.

"I wish. But they aren't hiring. I work at Big Scoop, the ice cream shop."

"I bet you get to see a lot of your friends there while you're working."

"And they get to see me in my ridiculous little hat and short skirt. It's so embarrassing."

"Then why . . ."

Maggie's face crumpled. She looked like she might burst into tears. Victoria should have bitten her tongue. She wasn't so rich or so clueless that she didn't realize some people didn't have as much money as she did. Like Cindy, for example.

"Never mind. Let's go," Victoria said, shifting her backpack to one shoulder. "After the day I've had, I need some serious retail therapy. And an ice cream cone."

seven

Rest is a good thing, but boredom is its brother.

—Golden Gate Fortune Cookies
(Not your mother's cookies)

Victoria was looking forward to having the house to herself, but when she got home from the open-air mall with its flower beds all in bloom, ferns and sculptures, and crowds of expensively dressed wives of Silicon Valley CEOs shopping at Pottery Barn and Williams-Sonoma, she felt a pang of unexpected loneliness. She reminded herself she was glad her parents left. That she liked being alone.

The trouble was the house was just too big for one person. The high-ceilinged foyer alone could have housed a whole family.

She set her Neiman Marcus, H&M and Bloomingdale's

bags filled with shirts, sweaters, shoes and boots in the solarium where sun still shone through the tall windows.

In the kitchen there was a pot of soup on the stove. She lifted the lid and inhaled the rich smell of dill and simmered beets. On the granite counter was an apple pie with cinnamon and butter, still warm and fragrant and oozing juices. There was a note from the housekeeper saying she hoped Victoria liked it and the note was signed *Jillian.*

Victoria hadn't had a chance to meet her yet. But her parents had interviewed her and were convinced she was just the person they needed.

"She comes with excellent recommendations," her mother said. "I feel much better about leaving you here now."

Did her mother tell Jillian that Victoria loved apple pie and borscht? Or was it just a coincidence that she'd made her favorite things on a day when she needed a little comfort food? So not only did the housekeeper supervise the gardeners and the lawn maintenance men, order the pesticide service and the tree care professionals, and find a pool service company, she made soup and baked pies too.

Victoria picked up the phone and dialed the number of the apartment above the garage.

A man answered.

"Uh, is Jillian there?"

"Who's this?"

"Victoria Lee."

A long silence.

"I can call back if this is a bad time."

Another silence.

"Hold on. Mom, phone for you."

No one had told her Jillian had a son. Maybe it was his job to screen her calls.

"Jillian, thank you so much for the soup and the pie. You don't have to feed me, you know. That's not part of your job. I can get food for myself."

"I was making soup for us and I thought you might like some."

"I love borscht. It's my favorite soup. There's this place in Hong Kong where I always order it, called Queen's Café . . ." Victoria felt a wave of longing for the dim, cozy, wood-paneled restaurant where she and her friends would meet for dinner on Friday nights to talk and gossip and just hang out. Then they'd go see a movie and laugh or cry from the front row. On Saturdays they'd do their makeovers—hair, skin and nails—and try on new clothes. Did girls do that here? Just dinner and a movie with their friends? Or did they all have dates?

Whatever they did, they hadn't ever invited her along.

Would she ever have friends like that again anywhere? "Anyway, I appreciate it."

"You must miss your parents."

"Oh, sure." *But I don't miss being reminded of who I am and what's expected of me 24/7. I don't miss hearing how lucky I am to be at Manderley. I don't miss them leaning over my shoulder every waking minute, choosing my classes and my friends and my future for me.*

"If there's anything I can do for you . . ."

"No, no." *Just teleport my old friends across the ocean for me.* "Are you settled in okay? Is there something I can do for you?"

"We're fine."

She must mean her and her son.

"Well, good." Now that everyone was fine, Victoria didn't know what else to say. She ought to be used to having servants by now, after a whole lifetime of being waited on by the staff who'd been with her parents for years, but this was different. This woman sounded like she could be her friend. Maybe that wasn't possible under the circumstances. Too awkward on both sides.

Victoria glanced out the window at the apartment over the garage. From an open window she saw a stream of soap bubbles float into the air. She blinked and the bubbles were gone. It must have been an illusion, a trick her eyes played on her, or even a hallucination from lack of sleep and the stress of dealing with her parents for the past two weeks. Sure, that's what it was.

eight

If you took all the students who fell asleep in class and laid them end to end, they'd be a lot more comfortable.

—Golden Gate Fortune Cookies
(Surprise your friends with a personalized cookie!)

The next morning Gabe headed off to school on his bike, determined to find out how he'd gotten into Manderley and who was paying for him. Since his mother refused to tell him, he had to think of another way. All he had to do was to go to the school office and ask, right?

He'd just pulled out of the driveway on the custom bike he'd bought used and rebuilt himself when a black BMW raced past him and almost ran him down.

The driver stopped, opened the window and stuck her head out.

"Sorry," she said, "I didn't see you." He was right. It *was* her, the beautiful but totally "I'm hot and you're not" girl from his art class and chem lab who'd called on the phone. Her mouth fell open. "What are you doing here?" she asked.

"I live here," he said, arranging his features in an expression of supreme indifference. He could be just as big a snob as she was. A reverse snob, but still a snob.

So what if she lived in the big house all by herself while he and his mother shared the small apartment. He wanted to tell her he had just as much right to live in San Marco Hills as she did, even though she was rich and he was poor. But he was too hip for that and he couldn't let his mask of coolness slip.

"Here . . . where?"

He pointed to the garage.

"You're Jillian's . . . ?"

"Son."

"You go to Manderley?"

Duh. He was in two of her classes.

"You're confused, I get that," he said. "You're asking yourself, how can a housekeeper's son afford the tuition? Well, I'm asking myself the same thing." Now why did he blurt that out? Her face turned pale under her skillfully applied makeup and she bit her lower lip, which was the color of ripe plums and just as full. He stared at her mouth, almost tasting the sweet, juicy flavor of the fruit.

Maybe she really was a model after all. Did that explain why she was so dense? Or was she just so out of touch with reality she couldn't believe he could be allowed to go to her school? Come on, he wasn't the only economically challenged kid at Manderley, was he?

"Do you want a ride to school?"

"In that gas-guzzler?" he asked, jerking his gaze from her flawless face to the smooth exterior of her car. "Do you know what carbon dioxide emissions are doing to the atmosphere?"

"Not really."

He shook his head in disgust. "That's what's wrong with the world. People like you have no idea what damage they're doing to the earth in a million ways. You drive your car instead of biking or walking. And when you drive, it's not a hybrid or a diesel or some other fuel-efficient car. Not for you. Oh, no."

She stared at him as if he'd wandered in from the nuthouse. He hadn't meant to go off like that, but how else were people like her going to get the message? From the startled look on her face, all this was new to her. She probably hadn't even seen *An Inconvenient Truth*.

All he wanted to get across was that he would not accept a ride in a car when he could ride a nonpolluting bike. That's all.

"So long, neighbor," he muttered with a sneer. Then he

took off and headed for school. With any luck he'd beat her there. That would show her. But even if it did, girls who looked like her and lived in a house like that had no reason to change their lifestyles. He was wasting his breath.

He left his bike in the parking lot between two giant SUVs. *What do you bet all that metal carried one incredibly rich and spoiled kid each to school by himself?* Gabe thought.

In the admissions office, which was located on the first floor of the former mansion of Gertrude Manderley, nineteenth-century poet and feminist, Gabe encountered a tall, red-haired student working there. She smiled at him. A student worker, and a friendly one. How rare was that? Finally he might have caught a break. She might even let him look through the files.

"I'm new this semester and I need to check on my tuition payments," he said briskly.

"I'm sort of new myself. What do you mean, your tuition payments?"

"I want to know who's paying for me to go here. I know it's not my mom."

The girl looked puzzled. Probably thinking, *Why don't you ask your mom? Or maybe it's your dad, did you think of that?*

"I don't know where you'd find that out," she said. "Maybe in the bursar's office, but not here. But I can tell you maybe it's nobody. Nobody's paying for me because I'm here on a scholarship. There are two kinds, need-based and merit-based. Both kinds you have to do work-study like I'm doing. Has anyone contacted you about a part-time job on campus?"

He shook his head.

"Then that's probably not it. Another way to come here without paying is to be related to a teacher. Faculty kids get free tuition."

"Really?" A lightbulb went off over his head. Faculty kids. That was it. His dad could be a teacher here at Manderley. Why else would his mom want him to go there? To force his father to acknowledge him. How else could she have connived to get him in without paying for it? But which one? The crazy art teacher? Was that why Gabe was good at art, because he'd inherited it from Julian? Or was it the jolly "science is fun" chem teacher? He could just see it now.

"Dad, I'm your son."

"Yeah, I know. Good to meet you. Welcome to my world."

"Thanks, Dad. Sorry I didn't get your 'science is fun' out-there personality, but I inherited your love of doing experiments. Whaddya say we team up and win a Nobel Prize for curbing greenhouse gas emissions?"

No, as much as he'd like to have a science guy for a dad, he couldn't see his mother falling for Mr. K. Unless he had been totally different seventeen years ago.

"Do you have a list of all the faculty?" he asked the girl. All he had to do was go down the list, and bingo, some name would ring a bell, and he'd find the man his mother was keeping him from.

"Sure," she said. She reached into the files and handed him a printout. He scanned the names but nothing rang a bell. Nobody said it was going to be easy. There must be another way.

nine

Show me a girl who's a good loser and I'll show you a girl who's playing pool with her boyfriend.

—Golden Gate Fortune Cookies
(Eat here or take out)

Victoria knew one way to see more of Steve, since it wasn't happening in English class, (in fact he wasn't even there today) and that was to go to the next water polo game. In the school newspaper, *Manderley in Motion,* there was a photo of the team and there he was. Fortunately, or unfortunately, his tight-fitting Speedo was covered by a school pennant. There was even an interview with him, which she quickly devoured while sitting on the Stuart and Evelyn Spikings Memorial Redwood Bench before she went to the game.

"Steve Heller, third from the left, is no stranger to winning. Last semester he played guard on the basketball team, which, although they didn't get to the finals, still beat arch rival Our Lady of Perpetual Mercy in the parochial league. When asked why he switched to water polo, Steve said, 'I've been swimming since I was a little kid. Last summer I had the good fortune to attend the Stanford Water Polo Camp where I learned a lot.'

"When asked if he was embarrassed to be seen in those tiny, sexy European-type Speedo suits, Steve only shrugged. But he did share with this reporter the reason he plays so many sports. 'In my opinion, sports prepare kids like me for the challenges that lie ahead in life. I've learned sportsmanship, teamwork, and above all a sense of self-confidence thanks to the role models like Coach Buckingham that I've met while playing various sports.'

"To see more of Steve, come and cheer the Sharks to victory on Thursday when they'll be playing the Sacred Heart Raptors in the Bill Barkley Memorial Pool."

Victoria was impressed. She didn't know Steve was so articulate. She knew he was a great athlete, that was no secret. Last semester she'd cheered him on on the basketball court, where he'd scored point after point against other private schools without breaking a sweat. He'd told her that because of his athletic ability he'd have his pick of colleges even if his grades went into the toilet this year.

She hadn't seen much of him last semester after they went

to the Welcome Dance together. She thought they'd had a good time, though she'd refused to freak dance with him. Not exactly refused, she just managed to escape into the bathroom where he couldn't find her until the headmaster interrupted the dance, threw out the DJ and began playing old-fashioned music from some other era like the '80s.

Maybe she should have given freak dancing a try. You can't avoid simulated sex on the dance floor if you want to date a popular guy like Steve, she told herself. The only time Victoria saw Steve after that was during their tutoring sessions, which he often canceled if he had a practice or a game. So all she had to do was let him know she wasn't the uptight virgin he thought she was.

She would give it one more try. A guy like him was worth it. She had to learn more about the sports so the games wouldn't be so boring. Pay attention to the action so she didn't start daydreaming. That was just the start. Then she had to learn to flirt. To play games. To read guys. To figure out what they wanted and give it to them. But how?

Steve was the kind of guy she'd dreamed of. The opposite of the guys she knew at home. The skinny ones with glasses who went to the all-boys school and belonged to the computer club, and who were definitely not into sports. No wonder she and her girlfriends had hung out by themselves on Friday nights.

Steve was the kind of guy every girl dreams of, so the competition had to be fierce. But since when had she shied away from competition? She was Miss Junior Hong Kong. She'd beaten out hundreds of other girls. If she could do that, she could get the guy she wanted too. Because it was all about persistence, and you really never knew what would pay off in the end. Not until you tried.

ten

Sports do not build character, they reveal it.

—Golden Gate Fortune Cookies
(Because you deserve the best)

On Thursday Victoria took a seat on the bleachers of the outdoor Olympic-sized pool. If only she were good at some sport. Skiing for example. She could have gone to Tahoe and run into Steve by chance on the slopes.

What a great excuse that would be to design a whole winter sports wardrobe, not just some ordinary, form-fitting bibs and quilted jackets for the outdoors, but some really new and different après-ski clothes. No fur or sparkles or reindeer motif sweaters, she knew exactly what she'd make for herself and others. Something sophisticated but practical. She was tempted to reach into her backpack for her sketchpad while the idea was fresh in her head. No, she was there to watch the game.

When the team came out Victoria gasped at the sight of those tiny Speedo racing swimsuits.

Maybe it was her sheltered background, but she felt her face redden and her whole body throb and heat up when she saw Steve with his bare broad shoulders, his tapered waist and the tight Lycra suit that barely concealed anything at all. Oh, was he ever built. So that's what they meant by "if you want to see more of Steve . . ." How much more could she stand to see?

However she tried, she couldn't take her eyes off him, whereas he didn't even glance at her in the bleachers. What would she have done if he had? Waved?

The two teams were lined up on opposite goal lines. The referee was poised on the side with a whistle in his mouth. But some guy in street clothes came dashing to the pool holding something in his hand. He kneeled down, filled a jar with water and walked out. It was all over in a minute. But the referee got excited, blew his whistle and announced a delay in the start of the game. He asked if anyone knew who the guy was.

Yes, she knew. It was *him*, her chem partner, Gabe. She knew at once what he was doing. He was taking a sample so he could analyze the pH level of the pool water. Why? For optional extra credit, that's why.

Why should she care? She shouldn't. She didn't. It was none of her business if he wanted to make an ass of himself. She just sat there waiting, staring at the turquoise water, her hands clenched together in her lap.

After a few minutes the game got under way and Victoria wondered again why she was there. It was beyond boring to watch guys pass a ball back and forth as they swam up and down the pool. With the uniform black caps on their heads and their water goggles, she couldn't even tell which one was Steve anymore. The referee was constantly blowing his whistle and the play never stopped even when someone was ejected for foul play. She had no idea who was winning or what really constituted foul play. Who cared? She had thought she could at least fake an interest in water polo, but she just couldn't.

She got up and left the pool but she didn't know where to go or what to do. While everyone else was rushing off to their after-school jobs at the mall like Maggie, or to work in the office on campus like Cindy, or even just to hang out with friends, she was standing in front of the central kiosk reading an announcement of the drama department's production of *Annie Get Your Gun*, and a flyer about a mural painting competition for the new library. She had no one to go to the play with and she'd be no good at mural painting. She didn't really have time for any extracurricular activities anyway, and she didn't have time to watch other people's activities like water polo either.

She was still barely into *A Tale of Two Cities*. All she could figure out was that it was such a confusing story with so many characters and so many locations, she couldn't keep it straight. No wonder she was hopeless in class discussions. She was almost relieved when her big sister Brooke caught up with her.

"You're one of my community service projects," Brooke said, "but what are yours?"

"Uh, I don't know. Do I need community service?"

"Do you need community service?" Brooke looked at her as if she'd asked if she needed designer jeans or two-hundred-fifty-dollar Fendi shades. The answer was that obvious. "Vicky, I can't believe I heard you say that. Manderley is known for its passionate commitment to the betterment of humanity. What are you interested in, World Hunger, AIDS, Adopt a Family? There's always Adult Literacy or my personal favorite," she paused to let the full meaning sink in, "the Big Sister program."

"I don't know," Victoria said. They all sounded dismal.

"You'd better come with me to the quad and sign up for something right away. If you don't do some hours this semester, you'll have to do it all your senior year along with your SATs and your college essay. That's what I did wrong. Now

I'm paying the price by being stuck with you, in a good way of course."

Victoria didn't seem to have a choice. Not if she didn't want to screw up her senior year and get stuck being a big sister to some clueless junior like herself. In the quad a dozen tables were set up with volunteer students taking names.

"What about the Special Olympics?" Victoria asked, pausing at their table to look at their colorful brochure.

Brooke's lower lip curled. "I don't think so. You meet a lot of kids that way, but let's face it, they're all klutzes and some of them can't even walk let alone run or swim. Oh, sure they try, but they're handicapped, I mean challenged. Yeah, that's what I mean."

"But even though they're not very good, they can get something out of trying, can't they?" Victoria asked.

"I guess," Brooke said with a little shrug. "I just don't want to be around when they try. It's too depressing. Let's move along. Uh-uh, not Save the Redwoods. Those weirdos will have you camping in the forest and standing like a human shield while people come at you with a chain saw."

"But the trees are beautiful," Victoria protested. By now she was feeling so edgy she felt like saying no to whatever Brooke suggested and yes to everything else. "Aren't they worth saving?"

"I couldn't tell you. All I know is they're old and that's their claim to fame. As my dad says, 'If you've seen one redwood, you've seen them all.' " She took Victoria's arm and dragged her past the Adult Literacy and the Feed the Homeless booths.

"Oh, here we go. The car wash. That's fun. One of my favorites. Sign up for that."

Victoria had never washed a car in her life. If she had their chauffeur would have been offended. He'd think they didn't need him anymore. But she was in California now. It was embarrassing to have a housekeeper here for just one person. Especially a housekeeper with a son Victoria's age who was in her class. A son who rode his bike to school and lectured Victoria on the environment.

If her housekeeper had to have a son, why couldn't he have been a cute little toddler, the kind of sibling Victoria had always wanted, one who would come knocking on her door and ask for a cookie, one she could teach how to draw and make collages by cutting and pasting. She'd encourage him, she'd show him how to unleash his creativity so he didn't have to learn on his own the way she had. Never mind.

She wasn't going to have a cute little sibling. She wasn't going to have a sibling at all. It was too late. Her mother was totally involved in the family business with no time for more kids. Victoria could swear she heard her mother breathe a sigh of relief when Victoria left for California and she could get back to business full-time.

In chem class that morning Gabe had hardly said a word to her except, "Hand me the beaker." That was the good news. The less she saw of him, the fewer words they had to exchange, the better. After that harangue this morning, she never wanted to see him again.

He obviously thought she was a spoiled brat. So what? She had had to watch his experiment with the floating soap bubbles outshine her "collapsing can" and then she saw him stay after class to talk to Mr. Kashigian. It was beyond embarrassing. Didn't he care what people thought? Was anyone that oblivious? He must be or he'd never had made a scene in front of the whole school collecting that sample to check the pH of the pool water. No one knew who he was, thank God, but she knew *what* he was—a geek. She'd rather be a brat.

eleven

To get back at someone who wants to argue with you, agree with him.

—Golden Gate Fortune Cookies
(Like Grandma used to make)

The car wash was on Saturday in the school parking lot. It was a perfect day for it. Cool, sunny and windy. Aside from a downpour, what wasn't a perfect day for a car wash? They should be pretty busy. No one in that upscale neighborhood filled with McMansions would even dream of washing their own car.

"Business should be good," the junior class president announced to the throng of volunteers. "If there was a car wash in your neighborhood for a good cause, wouldn't you stop and drive your Porsche or your Hummer in?"

The volunteers cheered. The answer was yes. The temperature was in the high 60s and the dress of the day was tight denim shorts for the girls and blue sweatshirts with Manderley written in raised gold letters across the front for the guys. Victoria had talked her new friend Maggie and her old friend Cindy into washing cars with her.

Even though they both had real jobs on Saturday, they needed community service hours too.

Right away the three of them lucked out by being assigned to stand out on the road holding "Car Wash $15.00" signs to lure drivers in instead of being stuck polishing metallic surfaces or detailing leather interiors.

Without her glasses and wearing shorts, Maggie looked so much better than she had at school last week. Victoria still longed to get her a new wardrobe, but she didn't know Maggie well enough yet to offer to help her shop. Cindy was just happy to be away from her stepmother's spa and tanning salon for a day. She said Marco had promised to come by to have his new Lamborghini washed, a Christmas present from his grandmother in Italy.

Victoria wished she had a boyfriend to come by in his Lamborghini. Instead her neighbor came by on his bicycle to harass them.

She muttered, "Oh, no." Then she turned away and feigned interest in the actual car washing behind them and tried to ignore him. But he stopped in the middle of the street and glared at them, holding up traffic in both directions.

"Don't you know you're encouraging conspicuous consumption?" he demanded loudly.

Victoria couldn't ignore that. She whirled around. "It's not our fault people drive expensive cars, is it? All we're doing is washing them."

"All you're doing is wasting resources," he said, straddling his bike with both feet on the ground and bracing his arms on the handlebars. "Where do you think the water comes from?"

Cindy and Maggie looked at each other. They didn't have an answer. They just wished he'd go away. Victoria should have warned them about him.

"The Sierras, that's where. It has to be pumped two-hundred miles. Then it has to be purified. Water should be used for something besides washing your stupid cars and SUVs. But that's not enough. Then you add detergent to it and drain it into the Bay where it pollutes the water."

There was a long silence. Cars were waiting impatiently to turn onto the campus. Horns were honking. People leaned out of their car windows and yelled at him. Victoria's face was flaming. This was community service. They were being attacked for doing good work. It wasn't fair.

"If you don't mind, there are people waiting," she said, stifling the urge to tell him to buzz off and leave them alone.

"I do mind," he said. "I care about the planet, unlike some other people here."

Victoria put her hands on her hips. "We don't care about what you care about. For your information this car wash is for a good cause."

"Yeah, what's the cause? The junior prom?" he sneered.

Damn, he would have to ask that. Before she could think of a good answer, like food for hungry Romanian orphans, Cindy blurted out the truth.

"The junior class trip to Hawaii," Cindy said. Victoria knew she didn't know any better. She didn't even know who Gabe was. Lucky her.

Someone in a convertible actually got out of his car. "Hey, moron, move it," he yelled.

Gabe turned and gave him the finger.

More horns. More angry voices.

Victoria wanted to sink into the asphalt and disappear. But Gabe finally pedaled away.

As he rode down the street, Brooke came charging out of the parking lot.

"What's going on here?" she demanded, tossing her long, shiny hair over one shoulder like she was in a shampoo commercial.

"Nothing," Victoria said. "Just a traffic jam." She only hoped her friends would keep quiet about Gabe.

"It wasn't that prick who caused it, was it? The guy who transferred from Castle this semester?" Brooke said, shading her eyes to look down the street. "If he gives you a bad time again, just report him. He's the kind of guy I was talking about. He obviously doesn't fit in," she said with a pointed look at Victoria. As if she knew where he lived and blamed Victoria for his presence. Then she turned to look at Cindy and Maggie, giving them each a super-critical up-and-down survey. Who knew if they'd pass Brooke's stringent requirements?

"These are my friends, Maggie and Cindy," Victoria said firmly. Let her try to knock them in front of her.

"Uh-huh," Brooke said, as if they weren't even worth commenting on. Then she shifted her gaze to the departing Gabe.

"I think it's definitely him, the one who rides a bike to school. How lame is that? He must be poor." Brooke wrinkled her nose in disgust. "Too poor to afford a car." She said it as if being poor was like having leprosy, a condition that *might be* catching if you got too close.

Victoria almost blurted something about how the emissions from cars were destroying the atmosphere. And that although Gabe was poor compared to them, at least he had principles. But why would she say something like that? Brooke wouldn't care about Gabe's principles and why should she? She was at least doing community service by washing cars, which was more than Gabe was doing on a Saturday.

Brooke finally went back to washing cars and Victoria, Maggie and Cindy went back to waving at the incoming cars.

"Who was that?" Maggie said.

Victoria sighed. "That was Brooke, my big sister. She's, uh, supposed to advise me, help me adjust to the school. But so far she mostly tells me what not to do and who not to hang out with."

"I meant the guy on the bike. Isn't he your chem partner? I've gotta say, he might be poor, and he might be a pain in the ass, but he's cute too."

"You think so?"

"If he got a haircut he would really be hot," Maggie said. "You can tell he's totally into that environmental stuff. He wasn't faking it."

"I know," Cindy said. "I mean, who else could object to cleaning cars for a good cause? I actually thought he was going to come over here and turn off the water. Maybe we don't agree with him, but at least he's got the guts to speak up."

"He's got guts all right," Victoria muttered to herself. She didn't admire him at all. He was just trying to get attention, here or in class. Maybe he had a point to make, but he was a major show-off.

"He reminds me of someone," Maggie said. "I know, the new James Bond. I mean, if he got a haircut."

"Maggie, be serious. This guy is *so* not cool. He's a nut-case," Victoria said vehemently. "Haircut or not."

Both Maggie and Cindy turned to look at her as if she'd gone off the deep end. Okay, maybe she got carried away. They didn't know how he'd gone off on her for her gas-guzzler.

What was wrong with speaking out against him? Everyone else did.

"He's still hot," Cindy said.

Maggie grinned at them, revealing a mouth full of metal braces. It was the first time Victoria had seen her smile. Now she knew why.

It was just a smile, just a little joke between the three of them, but for the first time Maggie felt secure enough to expose her mouth full of braces. And best of all, Victoria felt like she finally had girlfriends she could joke around with, talk about boys with, even argue with. Even endure criticism from a bicycle-riding eco-freak like Gabe. Or the snobby comments from her "big sister." All this was really better than having a boyfriend. She'd never had one, and maybe she never would have one. But at least she had girlfriends. For now, that had to be enough.

twelve

Those who think they know everything are very annoying to those who really do.

—Golden Gate Fortune Cookies
(Fortunes for the favored few)

Parent Night was the next week. Victoria had no parents in town to visit her classes and listen to her teachers discuss how challenging and rewarding it was to teach Manderley's exceptionally gifted students (knowing full well they earned a fraction of what any of the parents did for that privilege). Her parents would miss hearing teachers explain how this class was the best they'd ever had, and how wise the families were to have selected this school, because the cachet of a Manderley education would open many doors for them and the connections they made there would last for the rest of their lives. Victoria knew if her parents had been there, they would have eaten it up. Along with the tiny buttery cookies and fancy coffee served by volunteers in Manderley Hall before and after the campus tour. No cheap donuts or watery coffee for Manderley parents.

She was very thankful her parents were not there and were instead halfway around the world. No matter how cool your parents were, they were bound to be a source of embarrassment when they set foot in your school.

Her parents would be the object of curiosity, one petite and still attractive woman who was once Miss Junior Hong Kong herself, and one all-American China expert who wouldn't hesitate to ask her teachers a lot of questions, and tell anyone who'd listen how smart Victoria was, raised to be bilingual and bicultural too. If anyone asked, and even if they didn't, her parents would recount how they'd met at Berkeley and now lived in Hong Kong, and how they wished they'd gone to a fine prep school like Manderley.

Victoria's volunteer job, which counted toward community service, was to stand outside along one of the lighted pathways on the campus with a few other students and answer questions like, "Where is the Marshall and Antoinette Jackson Humanities Building?" and "Which way is FloMo?" (the short form for the Florence Montgomery Theater).

Cindy's stepmother would be there, but not to attend any of

Cindy's classes. Instead she'd be following her *real* daughters' schedules, the twins Lauren and Brie. Maggie's parents would be there too, but separately, since they were going through an acrimonious divorce. Maggie could hardly talk about it without crying, so Victoria didn't ask her.

"Excuse me, which way is the water polo coach's office?"

That was a new one. When the attractive, well-dressed couple who oozed money and success stopped to ask her, Victoria had to look it up on the printout they'd given all the guides.

"I don't think Steve would want us to talk to the coach," the woman said to the man.

"Our son is sitting on the bench, Linda. Something has to be done about it."

"Maybe he's not as good as the other players," his mother suggested.

Or maybe he fouled out, Victoria thought. At least she'd learned that much from her experience watching water polo.

Even under the dim light Victoria could see the man glower at his wife. "With that kind of attitude no wonder he's struggling. Of course he's as good as everyone else. Better. Didn't we spend thousands to send Steve to the Stanford Water Polo Camp this summer? The coach doesn't like him and we're going to find out why. *If* we can ever find his office." Now he was glowering at Victoria.

"Sorry," she said, fumbling with the map in front of her. So these were Steve's parents. It made her so nervous she stood there for an eternity shuffling papers and looking for the list of faculty and their offices. They must think she was a klutz who didn't know anything, just when she wanted desperately to make a good impression on them. That way when they got home they'd say, *We met the most charming girl tonight . . . So helpful. Why don't you date someone like that?* "Oh, here it is, in the gym. Just follow the path . . ."

"We *know* where the gym is," the man said. "Our son plays basketball there." They walked off muttering something about her incompetence.

She was so upset she dropped her pamphlet, campus map and flashlight. Of all times, of all people. Fortunately they didn't know who she was, though she was wearing a name tag and a big badge that said, "Ask Me." Victoria hoped they were too wrapped up in their son's problems to catch her name. Steve's parents were probably really nice when you got to know them.

But it didn't look like she'd ever get to know them. He'd probably never even mentioned her. Even though he'd taken her to the Welcome Dance. Of course she hadn't mentioned him to her parents. If she had, they'd have wanted a complete family history along with his GPA and class rank.

She'd just picked up the stuff she'd dropped when an attractive young woman in a belted black leather coat and skinny black pants tucked into leather boots stopped to ask where the chemistry lab was. Everyone who passed was well-dressed; that was a given. But this woman was younger than most parents and she had a certain look about her that was unusual for the average Manderley moms, who looked like they bought all their clothes at Talbots.

"That's an easy question," Victoria said, "since I go there three times a week."

"Then maybe you know my son, Gabe."

Victoria froze. If her son was Gabe, then this woman was her housekeeper. She didn't know what to say. All she could think was . . . *Yes, I know your son, but I wish I didn't. My God, he is such a dumb-ass, I feel sorry for you.*

Can't you do something about him? Like send him to a military academy? Anything. Just get rid of him. Get him out of my classes and out of my life.

Oh, yes, he thinks he's God's gift to science, but what he is is a pain in the butt.

As you probably know, he's a complete nerd with no social sense at all, and yet you seem like a nice normal person.

Why don't you get him to cut his hair? Never mind. That wouldn't help his warped personality. Maybe it's better if he keeps his face covered.

But if he did cut his hair, he might be able to see things better, like the world around him.

"Yes, I think I do know him," Victoria said at last. She took a deep breath. "I'm Victoria Lee, your, uh . . ." Now what should she say? *Your boss? Your boss's daughter? Your neighbor? Your son's lab partner? Your son's worst enemy, you know, the girl who's single-handedly ruining the environment?*

She didn't have to say anything. Gabe's mother smiled warmly and said, "Hi, Victoria. I'm Jillian. I've been meaning to come over to introduce myself. It's good to finally meet you. So you and Gabe are in the same chemistry class?"

"That's right." *I'm stuck with the pompous brownnosing moron every day for an hour.* If he hadn't told her they were partners or that she was a prime guilty polluter of the environment, Victoria wasn't going to either. "The chem lab is right down this path and to your right. You can't miss the teacher, he'll be wearing a 'Science is Fun' shirt."

"And is it? Fun, I mean."

"Not for me, I suck at science. But your, uh, son Gabe seems to like it. He's very smart." *Just ask him and he'll be glad to tell you. He thinks he's the next Stephen Hawking. He's the biggest show-off in the whole class. But you're his mother; you're probably proud of him. Used to him. You probably haven't even noticed he's an obnoxious prick.*

"That's nice to hear. Gabe loves chemistry," Jillian said.

Oh, that's news, Victoria thought.

"He's always loved mixing things together just to see what happens. I can't believe you really suck at science, but if you do, he'll be glad to help you."

Oh, right, he'd be glad to lecture her on his favorite topic. She would rather eat sea slugs than ask him for help. She knew what he'd say: *I don't help brainless rich girls. That's beneath me. If I'm going to volunteer I'd rather dig ditches or take care of AIDs patients.*

"I'll remember that," Victoria said.

"And if you need anything at all, just let me know."

Victoria nodded and watched her walk away. Then she turned back.

"Oh, by the way," Jillian said, "Gabe is an artist of sorts. He's into murals these days and I was wondering if your parents would object if he painted one on the inside of the garage wall."

"A mural?" She could see it now, some splotchy, depressing mess that was supposed to represent global warming. Who cared? No one would ever see it. "Fine. Go right ahead."

"Thanks."

Victoria wondered if Gabe wanted to paint the wall or his mother wanted him to. She knew what it was like to have your mother plan your life for you. She watched Jillian walk toward the chem lab, thinking she sure was different from the other parents, more hip and friendlier. Of course she wasn't as rich as the other parents. She was a housekeeper and Victoria knew exactly how much she made.

Later, after she'd stopped by the Multiple Use Room (MUR) for a cookie, Victoria passed a classroom, now empty except for the teacher and a parent, huddled together over a sheaf of papers. The windows were open so Victoria could hear them even though they were talking softly.

She didn't know the attractive male teacher, but the parent was Gabe's mother. So yes, she *was* wondering who the teacher was, but why were they cozied up together when open house was over? What were they talking about?

It suddenly occurred to her, *How* can *a housekeeper's son afford to go to Manderley?*

thirteen

When someone says, "It's not the money, it's the principle of the thing"—it's the money.

—Golden Gate Cookies
(Tasty, tempting and terrific)

It was Friday night and Maggie was working at Big Scoop in the mall. She didn't mind. That way she had an excuse for not having a date. Victoria didn't have a date either, but she said she still had to read *A Tale of Two Cities*, which was a long, long book. Maggie's arm ached from scooping flavors like Irish Cream and Brazilian Coffee to the super-sophisticated crowd that frequented the upscale mall. No boring Rocky Road or chocolate-chip cookie dough for these Silicon Valley multimillionaires and their children.

She hated the disgrace of having to work at the mall when everyone else was out having a good time. What really hurt though was that Maggie used to be one of those children of multimillionaires, strolling through the mall with her friends, her wallet full of money. But that was before the divorce. Now not only did she have an empty wallet, she didn't seem to have any old friends left either.

She glanced at the clock. Only fifteen minutes to go. From out of nowhere came a group of young kids carrying balloons and crowding into the store with a harried looking man.

"We'll have sixteen double-dip cones," the man said, waving his hand at the children. "Tell the lady what you want, kids."

Maggie's heart fell. She had been hoping to leave work at eight to watch a fencing match at Stanford. She loved fencing. She'd started when she was small after seeing the *Star Wars* movies. She'd wanted a lightsaber but her dad had bought her a foil and a mask instead and taught her a few basic moves. She joined a club, took lessons and soon she started winning matches. Her mom wouldn't watch because she thought it was too violent, but her dad was proud of her.

Now she only saw him every other weekend, and when she did, he didn't ask her about her fencing. He only complained about how much money her mother spent. Which was why Maggie was here scooping ice cream, to make money for extras so she wouldn't have to ask her mom or dad for spending money. Manderley was expensive. If she had to leave she wouldn't be able to fence on their team. And if she couldn't fence she wouldn't have anything left in her life.

She had to show her dad she wasn't a big spender like her mom. As long as he paid her tuition she wouldn't ask for anything else. Like money for contact lenses or designer braces instead of the clunky cheap ones she had. If she scooped ice cream every night for the next year and didn't spend a penny she might have enough money to get rid of her mouthful of metal and order invisible clear aligners instead.

Maggie was pulled from her thoughts when every kid in the store started yelling out their orders and every one of them wanted two different kinds of ice cream on their cone.

"Mango sherbet and coconut. No, make that one scoop of Mountain Blueberry with Chocolate Decadence."

"Could I have mocha chip and chocolate mint? Wait, what's that?"

Maggie sighed. "That's black walnut."

"Ew, I hate nuts. I'll take one peach and one fudge ripple."

This happened over and over. She scooped faster, handing cones across the counter as quickly as she could, when a little girl dropped hers. She burst into tears, so Maggie gave her a new cone.

Just then she glanced up and saw a group of familiar-looking kids her age walk by. Manderley students. The two blond girls looked like Cindy's stepsisters, but then half the senior girls looked like them. The same blond hair, the same perfect skin, expensive clothes from the same stores and the same attitude. Sometimes it was hard to tell them apart.

One of the guys was Ethan, her once-upon-a-time best friend from childhood. That was until junior high when he realized hanging out with girls, especially her, was lame. While he drifted away she realized she had a major crush on him, which only got worse as time went by. She thought it would be better when she moved away and wouldn't have to see him coming and going from the house next door, but it was more intense. She blamed it on hormones and the fact that she still had to see him at school—and now this.

Ethan was hard to miss. Taller than the others, with a killer smile and a rangy athletic build, he stood out in any crowd.

Just the shock of seeing him unexpectedly made Maggie's hand shake and she dropped a scoop of mint chip into a half-empty bin of Chocolate Decadence, ducking her head, she tried to hide behind the counter. She didn't want anyone from Manderley to see her in her striped hat and totally dorky outfit.

Most of all she didn't want Ethan to see her. She might as well have a sign around her neck that said, "See, I'm a dork." Not only that, it would say, "I'm not like a normal rich Manderley student, I wear a funny costume because I need money and I have to work." Which he probably knew because their families had been friends before the divorce. Of course they'd dropped her and her mother from their social circle soon after. No more Christmas open houses, no more pool parties in the summer.

She knew what he was thinking. *Poor Maggie. How pathetic. Those braces. No wonder she never smiles. She's got nothing to smile about. Those clothes. Where did she get them, at Target? She's a mess. If she has to work, why does she work in the mall where the whole world can see how low she's sunk? Why doesn't she babysit instead and spare us the agony of seeing her behind the counter of an ice cream store?*

She ought to transfer to Castle, which is full of poor kids where she wouldn't stand out like a Romanian orphan somebody adopted. Or like a pair of cheap faux diamond stud earrings? She doesn't belong at Manderley anymore.

Maybe he'd heard the gossip and was telling everyone at school that her mother was drinking too much. That she couldn't get a job because she was too depressed. That was probably a juicy topic around the dinner table at Ethan's house.

As for her father and his relationship with Ethan's family, she didn't want to know. Did her dad get invited over for drinks when they'd talk about what frivolous spendthrifts she and her mother were? How they were sucking him dry while he had to work night and day to support them?

With any luck the group would walk right by. They'd probably been to the movie theater next to the mall and were on their way to one of the cool hangouts with their fake IDs.

The good news was they wouldn't be so uncool as to stop for an ice cream cone.

Except, apparently, they were. At least Ethan was. But he didn't stand in line and wait to be waited on. Instead he edged through the crowd of kids right up to the counter.

"Busy night?" he asked, his hands on the glass.

She looked up and gave him a weak smile. "Kind of."

"Want some help?"

"Help? Oh, no, I'm fine," she said as her hat slipped off her head and fell into the raspberry sherbet.

"Hey, I got cherries in mine," a little boy said, waving his cone in the air so violently it fell on the floor and he stepped on it. "I hate cherries."

Maggie said she was sorry and replaced his cone with oatmeal cookie crunch.

Before she could stop him, Ethan ducked under the pass-through, came behind the counter, grabbed an ice cream scoop and started dishing out cones as fast and effortlessly as if he'd been doing it all his life. As far as she knew he'd never had a job of any kind, never needed to make extra money, never scooped ice cream professionally or done anything else besides the usual team sports.

Fifteen minutes and what felt like a lifetime later, every kid had a cone. Maggie had collected the money and she was ripping off her hat and apron, tossing them in a bin and turning off the lights.

"Thanks," she said breathlessly to Ethan. "I couldn't have done it without you."

"Sure you could."

"Maybe, but I'd still be doing it."

"Going somewhere?"

She looked at her watch. "Uh . . . I'm not sure. What about you? I hope you didn't lose your friends. Oh, there they are."

Across the way in front of the J. Crew window filled with preppy cardigans, little black halter dresses and cashmere pullovers Maggie could no longer afford, the two blond sisters were beckoning to Ethan.

"Over here," they called.

"We're going to meet some people. Want to come with us?" Ethan said to Maggie. He said it so casually he couldn't possibly mean it. He'd virtually ignored her for the past four years. Now he was suddenly inviting her to join him and those man-eating twins? Hah!

"Can't," she said. "I've got plans."

"Okay. Bye, then." He shrugged and walked away.

Maggie heard the twins shrieking as she left the mall. She thought she could hear them asking Ethan, Who was that poor wretch and why is she working there? My gawd, what an outfit! We almost died laughing. Honestly, I'd kill myself before I sold ice cream. What's wrong with her anyway? I hope no one saw you speak to her, Ethan.

All the way home she could hear their voices in her head. She could still hear the shrieks and she could still see Ethan coming to her rescue like a knight in shining armor, scooping ice cream next to her.

She hadn't spoken a word to him in weeks, not even "hey." They were in the same chem lab but they might as well be in different worlds. If she'd gone with him and his friends tonight would they have talked about chemistry, or about the past when they lived next door to each other, played together, swam in his pool, climbed up to her tree house? Hardly. He'd probably forgotten all that.

But because she hadn't taken a chance, she'd never know what they might have talked about. She wiped away a tear as she drove slowly back home.

fourteen

Life is like a buffet: It's not very good, but there's plenty of it.

—Golden Gate Fortune Cookies
(Click here to order your sample pack)

"Victoria, your house is beautiful," Cindy said, her head tilted back to admire the high-ceilinged great room with its hand-carved Chinese screens and framed scrolls on the walls.

"Thanks. It's bigger than the flat my parents live in in Hong Kong, but they wanted to put some money into California real estate as an investment. It's way too big for me as you can see. But what can I do?"

"I said this before, but now I'm sure. You should have a party, that's what you should do. Invite Steve."

"Wait a minute, doesn't that go against everything in the *He's Just Not That Into You* book?"

"That's possible," Cindy admitted. "But how will you know unless you try? My sister Brie would say go for it. That's the girl who's bagged every guy on the entire basketball team."

Victoria gasped. "Every guy?" she asked, thinking of Steve.

"Pretty much," Cindy said. "At least that's what she said before she stopped speaking to me. Whatever. I think you should be honest. Let Steve know you like him."

"I can't just go up and ask him. I haven't talked to him. He hasn't called me. He's in my English class, but he comes late and leaves early. Or he doesn't come at all."

"Send him an Evite, along with everyone else. It's not like asking him to a movie or something. This is a party. You'll be inviting all kinds of guys."

"I will? I don't know lots of guys."

"Doesn't matter. Everyone wants to go to a party."

"Even if they don't know me?" Victoria asked.

"Especially if they don't know you. You're a mystery."

"How do you know all this, Cindy?"

"The twins."

"I thought they weren't speaking to you."

"They're not. But they talk to each other and I can't help hearing. Blah blah blah. They've had so many boyfriends, they know how to get them and dump them. Sometimes on the same day. They also know what to do when they get dumped.

They've had lots of parties. Always when my stepmother is out of town, of course. I know more than I want to about that kind of stuff."

"Do you go to their parties?"

"Are you kidding? They hate me. Even more since . . . you know. I hide in my closet. They still have to drive me to school because their mother doesn't want to take me or buy me a car, so every day I'm stuck in the backseat of their jeep, listening to them rehash every sordid detail of their scummy little lives. That's how I know everybody wants to go to a party, especially if there won't be any parents there."

"Okay, I'll do it. But you have to help me. Come into my room and we'll get to work on your hair."

Victoria tossed a drop cloth over the thick blue and cream carpet in her room and instructed Cindy to sit in front of her three-way mirror on a straight-back chair. When she gave Cindy a thick fashion magazine to look at, Cindy giggled.

"Honestly, this is like a salon. A high-class salon. I love your room. Those pictures on the wall, where did they come from?"

"I drew them. I told you I love clothes."

Cindy got up and went for a closer look at the color prints of models wearing the latest fashions. "They look professional. You're good, you know. You're amazing. What are you going to be? An artist or something?"

"I'd like to be a dress designer. But it's a crowded, competitive field. I probably don't have a chance. But that's my dream job."

"The only designers I know are Ralph Lauren and Isaac Mizrahi. Are there any women?"

"Sure, there's Stella McCartney and Vera Wang and lots of others."

"There's got to be room for one more, Victoria."

"I don't know. If I'm serious about it I should go to a design school, but my parents would never approve of anything so frivolous. They have other plans for me. What about you, what do you want to do?"

"I'll tell you what I *don't* want to do. Work at my stepmother's spa when I graduate from Manderley. She told me I could be a masseuse or her accountant. She expected me to fall all over her with gratitude. All I can say is it's not going to happen. When I turn eighteen I'm going to college and I'm out of there. For good."

Cindy sat down again and looked around the room. "Some day I'm going to have a canopy bed like this and a window seat. What a life, Victoria. It's like a dream."

"It's not all what you think," Victoria protested, hearing a note of envy in Cindy's voice. "Sure I've got the house but I have to take care of things like paying the bills and . . . and . . . stuff like that. You don't think I'm a spoiled brat, do you?"

Cindy swiveled around to face her friend. "Of course not. You're on your own here. You take care of yourself and the house too. You're amazing."

"I have help though," Victoria admitted, glancing out the window toward the garage. "The housekeeper does a lot. She cleans the house, even makes food for me sometimes, calls the pool service or the tree-care guy and the pesticide service. Actually I don't do a whole lot. Maybe I should."

She looked at Cindy's reflection in the mirror. "Right now I'm going to make you over." Victoria rubbed her hands together. "Sit down. Relax and put yourself in my hands. You won't be sorry."

fifteen

A makeover is only skin-deep.

—Golden Gate Fortune Cookies
(Create a moment of pure indulgence in your day)

An hour later, Victoria put her blow-dryer down and smiled with satisfaction. Cindy looked stunning.

Cindy ran her hand through her short, layered, red-gold curly hair, jumped up and hugged Victoria. “I can’t believe it’s me. You’re a magician.”

The subtle dusting of bronzer over a light base covered Cindy’s freckles but didn’t make her look “made up.” A touch of mascara made Cindy’s eyes glow. Or maybe it was just because she knew how great she looked.

Victoria cocked her head to one side and nodded her approval. Her friend looked stunning, tall and willowy with stylish gleaming auburn curls. Victoria could just see her walking down a runway wearing her own designer clothes. A moss green cashmere sweater with an Empire waist, or maybe a silk chiffon capelet over a black camisole and wide-legged pants.

"Wait till Marco sees you," Victoria said. Marco was the type of guy who'd appreciate Cindy's hair and the kind of clothes Victoria would design for her someday.

"Hey," Cindy said, standing at the window. "Who's that?"

Victoria went to the window to look, but she already knew who it would be. "That's my neighbor."

"The guy who gave us the lecture the day of the car wash? You didn't tell us he lived around here."

"He lives above the garage with his mother. She's the housekeeper."

"What's he doing out there?"

"Who knows? Probably collecting samples of radioactive dirt for a chemistry experiment."

"I thought you were his partner. Shouldn't you be doing it too?"

"I am his partner, but not because I chose him. We got assigned. God only knows what he's doing right now. It probably has nothing to do with the class. He goes off and does his own thing. Extra credit or just for fun. If you call that fun, which I so don't. You heard what he said. He thinks I'm evil because I washed cars."

"He didn't say that."

"But he thought it."

"I gotta go, Victoria. Thanks again."

"You're sure I should have a party?"

"Absolutely. If I had a house like this all to myself, I'd have a party too. I'll bring Marco, and he'll bring some of the other soccer players. And you'll invite Steve; that's the point. He'll be flattered, you'll see. He probably has no idea that you're interested in him. Here's what I think. Guys are just as insecure as we are. Sometimes they need a jab in the ribs or a knock on the head."

Victoria took a deep breath. "Then I'll do it. How about a week from Friday?"

Cindy nodded and Victoria walked her to the front door. She watched Cindy walk across the lawn, then she saw her stop and talk to Gabe. What was she doing that for? Didn't she know he disapproved of her too? Cindy was just as guilty as Victoria of wasting water and polluting the ground water with detergents. Cindy glanced back at her and Victoria jumped behind the curtain. She didn't want Gabe to think she was watching him. But she thought she saw him smile at Cindy. He'd never smiled at her. What could they be talking about? It couldn't be her, could it? Not if he was smiling.

sixteen

Now is not the time to try something new.

—Golden Gate Fortune Cookies
(You pick the flavors!)

Victoria sighed. Another ho-hum day in chemistry. No matter what Mr. K said, science was *not* fun. No matter how many "fun" experiments they did with dry ice and crystals, Victoria only went through the motions. Unfortunately her lack of interest showed, because she'd gotten a D on the first quiz. Her partner didn't seem to be enjoying chemistry so much today either, but she didn't see what his quiz grade was. Probably an A.

"These experiments are for kids. They're meaningless," he muttered, while measuring baking soda in a cup. "Reading invisible ink. What does he think this is, junior high? There's so much more we could be doing."

"Like what?" Victoria asked.

He brushed the hair out of his eyes. "Like measuring the particles of smog in the air."

"Doesn't that bother you?" she asked.

"Smog bothers everyone. It can cause lung damage."

"I mean your hair. How can you see anything?"

"I know what you're getting at. Your friend told me you cut hair. What are you, obsessed? If I wanted a hair cut I'd get one. I can see enough to write an invisible message with this stupid mixture." He waved the paper in the air. "Mr. K, we're done."

Mr. K came bounding back to their table, beaming at them. "Fun, wasn't it?" he exclaimed.

Victoria pressed her lips together to keep from saying no and hurting the teacher's feelings, or worse, endangering her grade even more.

In the back of the room a guy was bounding toward the door in a cruel imitation of Mr. K while everyone around him laughed. She hoped the poor teacher didn't notice. Where she came from teachers got respect whether they were weird or not. In fact, they usually were. Wasn't it better to have a teacher who was at least enthusiastic about his subject and wanted you to be too? She caught Gabe's eye. She had no idea what he thought. He was probably so involved in planning his next experiment that he didn't even notice what was going on around him.

"All right," Mr. K said, holding their paper up to the light to read the invisible message. "Have you two chosen your extra credit projects?"

"What about collecting some DNA samples?" Gabe asked. "And having them analyzed."

Where did he get that? Victoria wondered. If this was a joint project, he could have asked her. She didn't want to collect DNA samples.

"Sure, if your partner agrees," Mr. K said, glancing inquiringly at Victoria. "Remember, this extra credit work is about learning to work together, to share information. Collaboration. Teamwork. That's what science is all about."

Teamwork. Where had Victoria heard that before? She waited to hear Mr. K tell them science experiments would prepare them for the challenges that lay ahead in life. Give them self-confidence through role models. Him, for instance.

But he didn't. Victoria decided that no matter how uninteresting it was, if this was what Gabe wanted to do, he'd do all the work. Just like Brooke said.

"If you do DNA, the lab's going to do most of the work, so the two of you will have to write a research paper too."

"Fine," Gabe said before she had a chance to say anything.

"Before you decide, you might want to look through this,"

Mr. K said, holding out a brightly colored pamphlet called, not unexpectedly, "Fun Chemistry Experiments."

"I don't need to look, I really want to do the DNA thing," Gabe said, ignoring the pamphlet. Victoria picked it up and thumbed through it as if she'd find something so interesting she'd glom on to it. Sure, like that was going to happen.

Then she saw it. A tie-dying experiment using cotton and brightly colored dyes all made from chemicals you could order and mix yourself. She loved tie-dye. She'd once made a skirt out of a beautiful piece of tie-dyed fabric from Thailand that she'd bought at the Saturday flea market in Hong Kong. But make the dye herself? She'd had no idea it was possible. It would be totally cool to make her own design and mix her own colors.

"Here's something I'd like to do," she said.

Gabe's eyes widened in surprise. It was obvious he didn't think she had a shred of curiosity or brains. He leaned over her shoulder to see what she was looking at. He smelled like citrus and sandalwood. In a way, the smell reminded her of home.

"Sounds good," Mr. K said, and Victoria came crashing back to reality and chemistry class. "I'll put you down for DNA plus paper and the tie-dye experiment. That should help bump up your grades," he said. "But remember, this is extra credit. You can use the lab to do your work only after you've got your classwork done. And it has to be cooperative. Two experiments, but both partners work together on both projects. That's the way it is in a real lab. For all you know, you may both end up as scientists."

Victoria didn't roll her eyes, but she wanted to. She wanted to tell Mr. K that was just as likely as monkeys flying out of her butt.

"As you know I keep the lab open from three to five, so if you need extra time, you can work together whenever it's mutually convenient."

Victoria nodded, but she wondered for the tenth time if it wasn't too late to change partners. Gabe lived on her property. He was in her art class, her chem lab. Now they had to work together after school too? Not if she could help it.

When she saw the picture of the results of the tie-dye experiment, she imagined herself making her own unique colors and dying some fabric, making wonderful designs by tying the fabric together, hanging it out on a line to dry, and finally making a dress for herself. But the instructions only covered a small handkerchief.

Oh well, she'd start small in the lab right here after school and then take it from there. It sounded simple enough. She didn't need Gabe's help for this. She didn't want it.

"You really want to do this dye thing?" Gabe asked with a puzzled frown after class was dismissed and they were walking out the door. "What if it doesn't turn out like in the picture?"

"That's science. I know you think I'm a lightweight, but this is a real experiment. I'm going to see how fiber-reactive dyes interact with different fibers in fabrics. It's all about hue, saturation and brightness." She was glad she'd remembered that part. Maybe he was just slightly impressed. Or not. "So yes, I want to do it. Why, did you think I was faking it?"

"Girls always do," he said with a touch of bitterness that caused her to shoot a quick glance in his direction. His expression told her nothing. Maybe if he didn't have all that hair hanging in his face she'd get a hint. Was he talking about chemistry, enthusiasm or something else? Had he been involved with a girl once who'd "faked it"? If so, she didn't want to hear about it or even think about it.

"I picked something I want to do. Why is that so strange? It's not as strange as yours, checking somebody's DNA. What's the point of that? Are we going to go after some criminal? Free some innocent guy who's in prison? What?"

If he had an answer, he kept it to himself.

seventeen

Help, I'm trapped inside a fortune cookie factory.

—Golden Gate Fortune Cookies
(Best damn tasting fortune cookies I've ever had!)

"Victoria, this is Brooke." *Oh no, Brooke again.* This sister business was starting to bum her out. "Just calling to tell you I nominated you for class treasurer."

"What? Wait, I don't want to be treasurer. I'm not good at math. And you're not even in my class. Besides, I'm new. I don't know anybody. Who would vote for me?"

"Leave that to me. I'll be your campaign manager. I've got it all planned. We'll play up your Chinese side. Everyone knows Asians are whizzes at math. You'll tell everyone how smart you are and they'll believe you."

"I can't do that. Because I'm not, especially in math."

"Put a cork in it, Vicky. No negativity. Who's running this campaign anyway? Right now I'm writing your mission statement. Any ideas?"

"No, listen, Brooke . . ."

"When they interview you for the school paper, you'll tell them how you're going to help balance the school budget and increase the endowment."

"What?"

"Gotta run now, catch you later."

It was after lunch on a cool and beautiful sunny day. Victoria was sitting with her friends on the new artificial lawn that cost more than the entire gross national product of a small country, but promised to save on fertilizer and water. How would Gabe feel about that? Who cared what he thought anyway? Victoria put a half-eaten brownie on the grass wondering if real or faux ants lived on faux turf.

"What was that all about?" Maggie asked.

"My big sister, Brooke. You remember her. You won't believe this. She nominated me for class treasurer. Without even asking me. You heard me. I told her I'm not good at math. I can't even add two and two without an abacus."

"Wait, don't you handle all your parents' financial stuff here?" Cindy asked.

"That's different. They have an accountant. I run everything by him."

"Maybe he can help you when you're class treasurer," Maggie suggested.

"Yeah, how about this? 'A vote for Victoria is a vote for Stephen Lam, Victoria's family's accountant,' " she suggested.

Her friends laughed.

"Seriously, Victoria, you should think about this. An upperclassman volunteered to run your campaign? Sounds good to me," Cindy said. "You've got a good chance at it."

"But I don't want it," Victoria protested.

Her phone rang again. "Heard about your party," Brooke said. "I'll be there. And I'm bringing some friends. No parents, right?"

"Well, no."

"Another thing. In case you're waffling, being a class officer will look good on your college application. Wish I'd thought of it. And about your philosophy of student government, what will being class treasurer mean to you?"

Victoria looked at Cindy, who was vigorously nodding her head. She took a deep breath. "Uh, let's see. Being class treasurer will prepare me for the challenges that lie ahead in life. It will teach me sportsmanship and teamwork, and above all give me a sense of self-confidence." It was such a crock of shit, even Brooke must realize she was joking.

"Wow, that's great," Brooke said. "And I was thinking you should get some good pictures of yourself, sexy but nonthreatening at the same time, because you've got to appeal to girls as well as guys. Go to Kinko's and have them blown up to poster size—a lot of them for the campaign. And while you're there could you pick up my mom's party invitations?"

"I can't, Brooke, I'm really busy . . ."

"Thanks, Vicky. Just leave them in my student mailbox."

"That was Brooke again. She thought I was serious. Brooke thinks being treasurer will look good on my college application."

"I hate to say it, but she's right," Cindy said. "And maybe this sounds cynical, but I think being your campaign manager will look good on *her* college application."

"Not if I don't win. How will being a loser help either of us get into Berkeley?"

"Do you want to go to Berkeley?" Maggie asked.

"No, but that's another matter."

"No matter where you want to go, you have to write a personal essay. If you lose this election, you can say defeat made you a better person," Cindy suggested. "And taught you what's really important in life."

"Like . . . ?"

"Oh, I don't know. Family, friends, love, loyalty, honor. Pick one. Or two. Whatever. I'm telling you, college admissions directors love to hear how you've grown and what you learned. How you've changed. How you went through hell and came out a better person. So if you win, it's because you suffered first and finally won against all odds. So you see, it's a win-win situation. You can't lose."

"Wait. What do I learn from winning again? I already know how to screw up the books, lose the money, and forget to pay the bills."

"You learn responsibility. You were once an airhead, now, presto, you're class treasurer, managing thousands, making spreadsheets. That's what they want to hear."

"That's awesome. How do you know so much?" Maggie asked her. "Did you learn it all from your sisters?"

"Are you kidding me? I'll tell you what I learned from those sluts. How to fight dirty."

"You? Cindy? Fight dirty?" Maggie's mouth fell open in surprise.

"Yes, me. You didn't think I was going to lie down and take it after the dirty trick they played on me the night of the prom, did you?"

"When they told you your stepmother had a heart attack?" Victoria said. "They got rid of you so they could hit on Marco."

Cindy nodded. Her face was red. Her eyes narrowed. Victoria knew she'd paid them back big-time. Got them suspended and then got them benched from cheerleading, but she didn't know the details. Cindy would never admit it, but their treachery must have really hurt her.

"I thought they got kicked out of school," Maggie said.

"They did but my stepmother made a large donation to the new library building and got them back in. But she couldn't get them back on the cheerleading squad since it was disbanded."

"That must have stung."

"Oh, it did. Since cheerleading was their reason for living," Cindy said. "It all fell apart right after the catfight in the gym. The headmaster had to be called in to stop the mayhem."

"Wish I'd seen that," Maggie said. "I heard there was blood on the new floor of the gym."

"Yep. I was shocked when they came home that day covered with scratches and with huge hunks of hair torn out of their heads. I was almost sorry . . ."

"Sorry? Why should you be sorry? You didn't have anything to do with it," Victoria said. "Or did you?"

"I may have," Cindy said. "I knew what crap they were saying. I knew they were angling to be team leaders. I knew how they trashed their teammates. It was time the other girls found out. I just facilitated the process a little."

"And the drug bust?" Maggie asked. "They don't blame you for that, do they? You didn't put the weed in their car."

"No, but I didn't tell them about the sting either. I thought it was time they got caught."

"That was the day they got kicked out of school, when the headmaster searched all the cars, wasn't it?" Victoria said.

"They were kicked out, but just for a week."

"So have your sisters bounced back from these little setbacks?" Victoria asked.

"I saw them at the mall the other night. They looked okay," Maggie said.

"If you don't get up close you won't see the bald patches on their scalps. Or the welts on their arms," Cindy said. "Oh, yeah, the skanks are back but they're not cheering anymore. They never even blamed themselves for what happened. They already thought nothing was their fault and that they were the best. Too bad they didn't learn something like humility. Oh well. Maybe next time."

"Next time? What are you gonna do to them next?" Maggie asked, wide-eyed.

"Haven't decided," Cindy said.

"They must be furious you got Marco and they didn't."

Cindy nodded. Then she flopped down on the thick phony grass and closed her eyes as if reliving all that snarkiness had worn her out. Or maybe she was just planning future revenge, or dreaming about Marco, who, in the opinion of anyone with two eyes, was totally worth dreaming about. Victoria almost warned Cindy the grass would stain her linen capris, forgetting the grass was just plastic. Those pants once belonged to Cindy's stepsister, who'd tossed them out, so she really wouldn't have cared anyway. No one cared as much about clothes as Victoria, who was sitting on a loose-leaf binder to protect her chocolate lowrider pants. Just in case.

Maggie stared off into space, a fine line between her eyebrows. Victoria knew Maggie's parents were getting a divorce and that she was caught in the middle. Was there a way of turning that disaster into something positive? How was Maggie supposed to learn from that experience?

"If your sisters aren't speaking to you, at least they don't try to run your life the way Brooke does mine," Victoria said. "And she's not even related to me. She says helping me counts as part of her community service. I'm her favorite project. She can't understand that I don't need a big sister. And I don't need to run for office. She's gone way overboard." Victoria said.

"Hey, isn't that Steve over there?" Cindy said, pointing across the field to an impromptu Frisbee game.

Victoria stood, smoothed her Empire waist tunic and squinted. Finally she made out his tall, athletic body wearing shorts and a T-shirt. Her heart pounded. Why hadn't he answered her Evite? Why did she only see him when he was a player and she was a spectator?

eighteen

If everything seems to be going well, you must have overlooked something.

—Golden Gate Fortune Cookies
(Try them, you'll like them)

For once things went her way. Someone tossed the Frisbee toward their group and Victoria reached out and caught it. The first time she'd ever caught anything. Steve turned and came loping gracefully across the grass. Muscular and toned, he made everything he did look effortless. Swimming, running, dribbling a ball down the court. He had been a great dancer too at the Welcome Dance. She could have danced all night with him, if only she hadn't been too wussy to freak dance with him. If she had it to do over . . .

"Victoria," he said, reaching out and taking the Frisbee. "What's up? How've you been?"

"Fine, great," she said, smiling so hard it made her face hurt. She even felt weak-kneed in his gorgeous presence. "I caught your water polo game the other day."

"You did? Did you see where some dipshit almost made us forfeit the game by running into the pool area with a jar of something? Security came but the guy disappeared. I think it was a plot to sabotage us, put poison in the water, something like that. You didn't get a look at him, did you?"

"Uh, no. I had to leave early. But I'm sure it was nobody I know." God forbid anyone would think she was involved. Of course she did get a look at Gabe with the jar of water he was testing for the pH and bacteria. He'd told her about it the next day in class. Not that she wanted to hear about any of his extra-credit experiments. Honestly, the guy had no sense of shame. No idea he'd done anything wrong at all. He was a hopeless case.

"Anyway, you're having a party," Steve said. "Can I bring some friends?"

He was coming! She didn't care if he brought the whole water polo team. In fact, that would be great. Her party would take off. She looked down at Maggie and Cindy, who were pretending not to listen. They gave her a subtle thumbs-up sign.

"Oh, sure, of course." She heaved a sigh of relief. Whatever happened at her party, she didn't care as long as Steve would be there. It was worth the worry and the effort. He'd see her and he'd see her house. They'd have time to talk. He'd realize they were meant for each other. Just as long as his friends weren't Cindy's stepsisters. She could deal with neglect or too much interest, but she couldn't deal with evil.

nineteen

Don't hate yourself in the morning; sleep till noon.

—Golden Gate Fortune Cookies
(Experience the Golden Gate difference!)

The day of her party got off to a bad start. First Victoria's car wouldn't start. Then when she ran back in the house to call Triple A to come and jump-start it, she found her phone was dead. She went to the three-car garage, ran up the steps and knocked on the door of the apartment.

"Can I use your phone?" she asked breathlessly. "My car won't start, my phone's dead and my cell doesn't work here."

Gabe stared at her for a long moment. What was his problem? She'd asked to use his phone, not his toothbrush.

"What's wrong?" she asked. "Can I use it or not? I have to get to school early for my math help session."

"Okay," he said, stepping out of her way and waving his hand toward the phone in the kitchen.

Triple A said they'd be there in an hour. She told them she couldn't wait, that she had to leave now. She hung up and looked around the kitchen. She'd never seen it before. The counters were maple, the cabinets were white, and the floor was done in dark red Mexican tiles. She forgot her mother had supervised the redecorating of the apartment. Her mother really had excellent taste and plenty of money to spend on the best materials.

An abstract picture hung on the wall under a spotlight, all shapes and angles in contrasting colors that caught her attention. She stepped closer to study it. Her mother wouldn't have chosen that. Yet it looked right there.

"Interesting," she said.

"Think so?"

She turned to look at him, struck by the tone in his voice. "It's yours, isn't it? You did it."

"Yeah, why?"

"You're good."

"And you would know that because . . . ?"

She clamped her lips together to keep from snapping, *What's wrong with you?* Honestly, some people just couldn't accept a compliment.

"Okay, maybe I don't know anything about abstract art. So shoot me. I'm a hack who draws pictures of women wearing clothes. But I know what I like and I like your picture."

"Really."

"Yes, really." She stepped back. "Is your mom around?" she asked coolly.

"She's gone to her Pilates class."

She sighed.

"I have an extra bike. If you're desperate. Or don't you know how to ride one?"

"Of course I know how to ride a bike," she said. "Or did you think I rode in a carriage pulled by forty-eight matching white horses where I lived? It was Hong Kong, not another planet. People there get around like everyone else in the world."

"I thought maybe you had a chauffeur."

Oh, crap, of course they had a chauffeur, but he didn't have to know that. "I'd be happy to take a bus, but in case you didn't notice, there's no public transportation here, which is why I have to drive a car,' " she said.

"Not today," he said with a smug smile. She never should have knocked on his door. She'd have been better off calling a taxi or hitchhiking or crawling to school on her hands and knees. Anything was better than standing here begging for a ride to school and enduring his stupid comments. He was the most difficult person she'd met at Manderley, and that was saying a lot.

"Fine," she said. "I'll ride your bike." She knew she didn't sound very grateful, but she was too upset to fake gratitude. She just wanted to get this humiliating experience over with.

Gabe swung his backpack onto his back and led the way to the garage where he wheeled out a slightly worn but famous label racing bike and leaned it against the door.

"Follow me," he said, handing her a helmet. "I know a shortcut."

Wait, she wanted to say, *those wheels are too skinny. I'll fall over. I can't ride very fast and I'm afraid of the traffic.* But she wouldn't give him the satisfaction of saying *I told you so.* And thinking to himself, *Rich Bitch.*

She looked around the garage. "I thought you were going to paint the wall."

"Who told you that?"

"Your mom."

"Figures."

"So are you?"

"I thought you were in a hurry."

So he didn't want to talk about it. Fine with her. She would not say another word to him about art or anything else. Once they got to school, she was going to pretend she didn't know him.

Good thing she was wearing jeans today instead of a short skirt. She had to pedal like mad to keep up with him, but she didn't dare fall behind and risk getting lost or, worse yet, earning his scorn. He already thought she was a pampered weakling.

Who cared what he thought anyway? The worst part was when they got to the stop sign two blocks from the entrance to the school and were passed by all the students in their fancy cars who stuck their heads out the windows and yelled at them.

"Go, Lance," one guy called.

"Hey, you're late. The Tour de France is over."

"Let's race." This remark was accompanied by the accelerating of the driver's engine.

Victoria kept her eyes focused straight ahead, pretending she didn't hear the comments, hoping no one would recognize her under her helmet. Gabe either didn't hear them or was used to it. He didn't seem to mind.

"See," Gabe said when they pulled into the parking lot, "you got here just as fast as you would have in your gas hog. And you got some exercise too. You're not that bad a rider."

She might have gotten there just as fast and gotten exercise, but now the hair she'd carefully blown dry this morning was matted down from the helmet, and she probably looked like a total wreck. What if Steve saw her?

Not only that, she was out of breath and her muscles ached. And her face was probably flaming from taking in those rude comments. Not that she'd let Gabe know any of this. He'd just make fun of her. *Not that bad a rider.* Was that his idea of a compliment? Probably thought she'd be so flattered, she'd give up her car.

"Thanks," she said as he strapped her helmet to the handlebars for her. She leaned over and *A Tale of Two Cities* fell out of her backpack.

He picked it up and handed it to her. "You're reading this?"

She nodded. What, did he think she was illiterate?

"Of course I have trouble with the big words," she said.

He ignored her. Maybe he was afraid she wasn't kidding.

"Good book. I read it last year in my lit class at Castle. How do you like it?"

"I don't. It's long and I don't get it."

"You don't like science, you don't like books, you obviously have no interest in the environment. What do you like?" He was so close to her that she could see his brown eyes were flecked with green, like a piece of silk shimmering in the sun. She blinked and stepped back.

"What do I like? Believe it or not, I like abstract art." He thought she was a brainless, empty-headed idiot with no interests except herself. What was the point of trying to change his mind? She took a deep breath. "I also like my gas-guzzler car. I like going to European restaurants and kung fu movies on the same night. Because that's the kind of mixed up person I am. I also like doing makeovers for my friends. I cut their hair and I help them choose their clothes. I especially like cutting people's hair when it hangs in their face. I know what you think. I'm a totally self-centered loser, but just to show you I care about something else, and *someone* else, I'll cut your hair for free as a public service for anyone who's unfortunate enough to have to look at you."

His mouth twitched. Was he going to laugh or lash out at her? Probably the latter. She couldn't imagine him laughing.

"There, I've told you more about me than you wanted to know. But you asked," she said.

"Okay," he said flatly.

"Okay, what?" she asked.

"You can cut my hair. My mom will thank you for it. She's the only one who has to look at it. But don't forget we're collecting DNA samples today at three."

"Three? No, I can't. Not today. I'm having a party tonight. I have to go home, get my car battery charged, go to the store and pick up some stuff."

"Wait a minute. You'd let a party interfere with our scientific research?"

"It's not 'our' research it's 'yours.' I never said I was free today. You should have asked me. We're supposed to cooperate, right? It's the scientific way. Thanks for the bike. I'll leave it at your house this afternoon. And if you're looking for something to do, why *don't* you paint something on that blank wall in the garage? Maybe you'll be famous someday and my parents will make a fortune charging people to look at it. Or if you'd rather, you should enter the mural contest the library's sponsoring. If you won, that would show that Eurotrash art teacher, Julian."

She walked away from him before he could tell her why he wouldn't or couldn't. Or to butt out of his life. She didn't want to talk anymore. It was clear he still thought she was a simpleton. She thought he was a smug environmentalist. Would he remember about their deal to cut his hair? She hoped not.

Would he paint the wall? Would he enter the contest? Not if it was her idea. She was the last person he'd listen to.

twenty

You will give a party where strange customs prevail.

—Golden Gate Fortune Cookies
(You pick the flavors, we supply the taste!)

It must be the quietest, dullest party anyone had ever had, Victoria thought. Nine thirty and out on the patio Chinese lanterns swung in the wind and heat lamps pumped warm air on Maggie and Cindy and three other girls drinking sodas from a large ice chest and nibbling on the bruschetta, grilled veggies and ceviche she'd picked up from the deli at Whole Foods once her car battery had been charged that afternoon. Maybe she'd tried too hard. Maybe she should have stuck with chips and dip.

The music she'd carefully chosen—some rock, some hip-hop, some dance music—was piped to the outside speakers from the console in the living room. Now if only there was someone to dance with. Steve, for example. If he didn't come, she'd be sorry she ever had this stupid party.

She tried not to keep looking at her watch and listening for the sound of cars in the driveway, but she couldn't help it. What good did it do to spend a half hour trying on three different outfits and another half hour on her hair and her makeup? Who was there to notice except her friends who always complimented her anyway?

All she needed was for some more people to show up. Actually all she needed was for Steve to show up. He said he'd come. She just had to be patient. Because he was definitely worth waiting for.

Cindy had assured her that Marco would come with the soccer team. That would liven things up. And it did. The guys were not of Marco's caliber, not as sexy, not as classy or as gorgeous, but no one was. He was Italian after all. Not only Italian but the descendent of a count or something. Now there were at least ten other soccer players and it greatly improved the girl-guy ratio. Victoria nudged Maggie into asking one of them to dance. A few more people came and soon they were dancing too.

Victoria was so desperate to get the party off the ground she was even glad to see Brooke arrive with her "posse," as she called the group of senior girls and guys.

"Nice place you've got here," she said to Victoria as she looked around at the house with lights blazing from every window. "This is where we'll have our victory party."

"Are you so sure I'm going to win?" Victoria asked.

"Of course. Wait till you see what I've got planned. Streamers, balloons, buttons and those fabulous posters. How did they turn out?"

"Uh, not so good." It was a shock to see her face blown up to poster size and her boobs the size of oranges. Actually, not hers. Somebody else's. Brooke was so proud of the job she'd done Photoshopping Victoria's head onto a well-endowed model's body. It was positively the last thing she wanted to post all over school.

"Oh, Vicky," Brooke said, "you're pulling my chain. I bet they're great."

"Instead of posters I was thinking I could get us some fortune cookies," Victoria said. "I know some people who own a cookie factory." Now why did she have to say that when she didn't even want to run for treasurer? Each word brought her closer to the point of no return where she wouldn't be able to escape.

"No kidding? Could we put our own messages in them?"

"Of course, that's what they do. Like, 'Confucius say you have heart as big as Texas.' "

"That would be so cool. How about 'Victoria for Treasurer,' or maybe 'Victoria's Secret—Confucius say she's our next Treasurer.' I love it. You're thinking big, Vicky, finally. I'm proud of you. Of course you wouldn't be doing any of this if I hadn't told you to."

"I know that, Brooke, this was all your idea, but here's the thing. I'm not sure I'd be any good at it. Being treasurer, I mean. I really suck at math."

"Ha, ha," Brooke said. "Like people are going to believe that? Just in case, don't say it," she said with a quick glance over her shoulder. "Don't even think it. It's all about appearances. Don't confuse the issue with an effort to be honest."

Victoria didn't know why she'd blurted out her idea about the fortune cookies. Oh, yes, it was to cancel the poster idea. She really didn't want to run, and she didn't want to win. She didn't want to go and buy a gallon of fortune cookies encouraging people to vote for her. On the other hand, they were a little more subtle than the X-rated posters which she had planned to spill paint on and render useless.

With any luck she'd lose the election and then use her loss as a subject for her college essay as Cindy had suggested. She'd lose, but she'd really win, because she wouldn't have to be the treasurer after all. But it would look like she'd tried. And she'd make herself into the world's greatest loser. She could only hope.

It was almost midnight, her feet hurt in her new slingbacks and she was about to give up on her lackluster party when she looked up and saw Steve walk onto the patio with a group of macho, loud-talking senior guys. For a moment her heart stopped beating she was so excited. She rushed up to say hello and he kissed her on the cheek. She smelled beer on his breath. Good thing he'd already had something to drink, because she wasn't serving alcohol. After all, she couldn't buy it legally. And she didn't want anyone to drive home drunk after her party and get into an accident.

Then she noticed someone had managed to buy a keg and had hauled it in and placed it on the redwood table in the middle of the brick patio. Was it Steve and his friends or Brooke's friends who'd brought it, or someone else she didn't even know? Should she complain? No, Steve would think she was some kind of weirdo.

In a matter of minutes her party had taken on a whole new atmosphere. The music was amped up so loud she couldn't hear anything else. The beer was flowing. Not only that but her living room was full of guys and girls she didn't know, who were drinking from a bottle of cognac they'd taken from her parents' liquor cabinet—and had already spilled some on the off-white carpet.

"Guys," she said, her eyes wide with alarm. "Uh, that liquor is off-limits. Sorry."

They just laughed at her and said it was a great party and they were having a good time. Actually they shouted to be heard over the ear-splitting music.

She stood in the middle of the room, gnawing on her fingernail, looking around helplessly and wondering what she was supposed to do now. Order them to leave? What would her parents say if they knew? Her phone was ringing. What if that was them? Had they installed a webcam? Could they see everything that was happening?

Maggie was waving her arms from the patio, trying to tell Victoria something, but she had no idea what it was about. The phone call was not from her parents. It was a neighbor complaining about the music. Victoria said she was sorry and she'd turn it down. They asked if she knew what time it was. She knew. She did turn the music down but when she went outside there was a huge crowd on the patio and the music was louder than ever. Who were these people and how had they heard about the party? Did they even go to Manderley? Her head felt like someone was pounding on it with a croquet mallet.

Cars filled the driveway. She didn't know a single person who had parked there and then stormed into the house like they owned it. Or like they'd been invited to the party.

Finally Victoria found Steve near the garage, surrounded by his friends who'd tossed their beer cans in the flower beds and were drinking from the set of diamond-cut crystal glasses from the wet bar in the living room. He didn't look quite as sexy as he did in class or at the pool.

She glanced up at the apartment above and wondered what Gabe and his mother thought. All the windows were dark. Maybe they were both out. Or asleep. But if they were they must use ear plugs.

She tugged on Steve's sleeve. "Could you come and help me for a minute?"

"Sure, Victoria," he said as he stumbled toward her and threw one arm around her shoulders. "Hella good party." She wrinkled her nose as he sloshed a glass of cognac all over her jacket and the sour smell hit her in the face. As they walked toward the house she thought either Steve had drunk an awful lot of her father's best Scotch or he'd drunk an awful lot of something else before he got to the party. She wasn't sure which was worse.

Victoria no longer wanted to have a "hella good party." All she wanted was for the guests and crashers to leave before the neighbors called the police.

It was a little quieter in the kitchen. "I don't know who they are," she said to Steve, who was slouched against the granite counter, "but would you do me a favor and tell the guys in the living room they can't drink any more and ask them to leave?"

Steve laughed loudly and slapped Victoria a little too hard on the shoulder. "You want me to break up the party? Come on, Victoria, we're all just having a good time."

"I don't think so," she said. But maybe he was right. Maybe this is what passed for a good time with the Manderley crowd. Still, she couldn't go along with it. "Someone broke into my dad's liquor cabinet and I don't even know who it was. I think everyone had better go home." She hated to hear herself sounding like a prim do-gooder, like some kind of dork, but at this point she had no choice. She just wanted it all to be over.

"We just got here," Steve said. He hugged her with one arm and kissed her. Then he stuck his tongue in her mouth. She shuddered and pulled back. This was what she'd been missing? He pushed her roughly against the counter.

She'd braced herself against the granite countertop. Sure, she'd wanted to be kissed. She'd wanted Steve to like her. But this wasn't how she'd wanted it to happen. To be trapped like a rabbit in her own house. His kiss was not romantic at all. It was too wet and too sloppy. What was wrong with her? She finally got what she wanted and now she didn't want it.

"Never mind," she said, trying to pull out of his grasp.

He shoved his hips against her and kissed her again. This time she felt a surge of revulsion. "Stop," she said.

He backed away. "What's your problem?" he asked angrily. "Thought you liked me."

"I thought so too," she muttered.

He gave her a stupid forced wobbly smile, then filled his glass from a bottle of brandy on the counter, spilled half of it on the floor, and said, "You're weird, you know that? And I'm outta here." Then he stumbled back to where his friends were gathered by the garage.

"What'll I do?" she asked Cindy when she found her on the patio and described the scene in and outside the house. "I can't get rid of anyone and I'm afraid the neighbors are going to call the police." She was holding back tears of frustration.

"That might not be a bad thing. That will get rid of those jerks out there. I guess it will get rid of everyone. But what about Steve? Do you want to get rid of him too?"

"Yes. No. I don't know. The problem is he's not himself. He's drunk." The only thing Victoria knew was she wanted to have the house to herself again. Her head was splitting and her mouth was dry. She felt her stomach heave even though she hadn't had anything to drink except a Diet Coke.

"I'm really sorry but I have to go, Victoria. Marco's waiting for me outside. We have to pick up his cousin at the airport otherwise I wouldn't bail on you. Just go turn off the music and tell everyone the police are coming."

"I will. Thanks for coming." Victoria took Cindy's advice and went to the living room where she unplugged the sound system. The sudden silence was a shock. When she went back to the garage she found two guys had passed out on the cement driveway, Steve was throwing up on the dahlias the gardener had just transplanted, and his other friends were leaning against the garage door. There was broken glass all over and the smell of vomit and beer filled the air.

"Oh, no," Victoria moaned. Then she pulled herself together. This was her house, her party, and most of these people were not actually her friends. Friend or not, everyone had to go.

"Okay," she said loudly. "The police are coming. You have to leave."

No one moved.

From above her a deep voice came out of the dark. "You heard her. Leave."

Victoria looked up. So did Steve. It was Gabe. He threw a bucket of water on Steve's head. Steve choked and swore loudly. "Hey, man, what'd you do that for?" he yelled. "I'm not going. Neither are my friends. Who's afraid of the cops?"

He grabbed Victoria and wrapped his arms around her so tight she couldn't breathe.

"Steve," she said through clenched teeth, "let me go."

"Relax," he said, "it's a party. Go with the flow."

"Let her go." It was Gabe who'd suddenly come up behind Steve and grabbed him by the shoulders.

Surprised, Steve whirled around. "What the hell?" He swung one arm at Gabe, who ducked. Then Gabe punched Steve on the chin and Steve staggered backward while Victoria jumped out of the way.

Steve put his hand to his face and turned pale when he saw the blood on his finger. Victoria blinked back tears. Sirens wailed. The party broke up fast after that. Victoria followed everyone out to the street as two black and white San Marco Hills police cars pulled up, their red and blue lights flashing. This was it. She was going to jail.

twenty-one

Cheer up, the worst is yet to come.

—Golden Gate Fortune Cookies
(Made from scratch)

Victoria was shaking. On top of hosting a loud party, she'd served alcohol to underage minors, and what if they knew about her dozens of parking tickets? What would her parents say when she called them from jail? What would her father say when he saw his cognac was gone? Why had she thought she needed a boyfriend? She didn't.

One of the policemen got out of his car. "Victoria Lee?" he said.

Victoria's knees buckled. She couldn't breathe. She thought she was going to faint. This was her last breath of freedom. She was going to be handcuffed and arrested and taken away.

And no one would bail her out. She was alone. If this had been Hong Kong it would be even worse. Her picture would be in the paper. Her whole family would be disgraced.

"Noise complaint," the officer said, reading from his clipboard. " 'Code 4955, Ordinance 2803, Section 55. Residential zone, unreasonably loud, unnecessary or unusual noise which disturbs the peace and quiet or causes any discomfort or annoyance to anyone living in the area.' " He shined his flashlight in her face. "Having a party?" he asked.

"Yes, I'm sorry. It's over now."

"Age?"

"Uh, seventeen."

"Parents home?"

"No, they're not.

"Figures," he said. Then he looked at the motley bunch of teenagers sitting, standing, lurching or crawling toward their cars. "Wait a minute," he barked. "No one is driving in an intoxicated state. Out of your cars," he shouted.

Victoria shuddered. No one had locked her up or even blamed her, but if they couldn't go home, where were all these kids going?

When three taxi cabs pulled up, she thought she must have been dreaming.

"Smart move," the officer said to Victoria. It was a smart

move, calling the taxis, but she hadn't done it. As if they were sheep, the policeman herded the kids into the taxis. It was all over in five minutes. Victoria didn't care what happened next. They could take her away and lock her up, but at least her party was over and she'd never have to have another.

"So," the officer said as the taxis drove away down the quiet, deserted streets of San Marco Hills. "The party's over. Everybody gone? Better check." He and Victoria walked back into the house and then out to the patio. There was no one left, just one big, huge mess of broken glasses, stained carpets and mashed flower beds.

"No more parties, young woman," the office said before he left, "without your parents home."

Victoria nodded. Was he actually going to leave without arresting her? Yes, he was. She sat on the front steps of the house, numb from head to toe, watching the police car drive away, trying to make sense of it all. She was free. Everyone was gone. What had happened?

twenty-two

Do or do not. There is no try.

—Golden Gate Fortune Cookies
(People will be talking long after your event is over)

Clunk, crash, crunch, crackle. The sound of glass breaking is unmistakable, especially after midnight in the quiet San Marco Hills neighborhood. Victoria jumped up and ran to the back of the house. There was Gabe, sweeping up broken glass and dumping it in a garbage can.

"Oh, my God, don't do that," she said. "I'll do it. It's my mess."

He stopped sweeping, leaned on the broom and looked at her. In the dim light from the Chinese lantern overhead his face was half in shadows. He looked older and more with it than any guy who'd been at the party tonight. Including Steve.

Especially Steve. Gabe must be disgusted by the whole scene, but he didn't look it. He looked mysteriously attractive. But after what she'd been through she was so tired that anyone would look mysteriously attractive to her at that time of night. Especially if they were sober.

Once again there was the faint smell of sandalwood in the air. Why didn't he say something? Why didn't she? Why did he just stand there looking at her as if she were an alien? Because she looked like a disaster had struck. Her skirt hung crooked and her jacket was wet and reeked of Scotch.

And because he was repelled by the behavior of her guests. So was she. She hadn't even invited him to her party, and yet he'd come to her rescue and she hadn't even thanked him for it.

"I'm really sorry about the noise and the mess," she said. "Hope I didn't keep you awake."

"No problem," he said.

"Thanks for stepping in and, you know . . ."

"Punching out your boyfriend?"

"He's not my boyfriend."

"It wasn't a fair fight. He wasn't sober."

"And you were." Because he hadn't been invited to the party.

"Right."

"The police came."

"Yeah, I know."

"That scared me. If this were Hong Kong . . ."

"But it's not. It's San Marco Hills where rich kids have parties all the time. Their friends drink too much, vomit, make noise, the neighbors complain, the police come and it's no big deal."

"Most of them weren't even my friends. I don't know who they were. What about your mom?" Victoria glanced up at the dark apartment over the garage.

"Spending the night in Napa."

Victoria breathed a sigh of relief. "Are you going to tell your mom what happened?"

"Are you going to tell yours?"

"No."

"Then I won't tell mine."

"Thank you. And thanks for encouraging the guys to leave."

"You mean the water torture?"

"Yes, that. Wait, was it you who called the cabs?"

"Thought it was a good idea."

"Very good. I mean it. I'm going to clean up this mess tomorrow."

"If you want to do it now, I'll help you."

She didn't know what to say. *Thanks* didn't seem like enough.

So she didn't say anything until they'd finished sweeping, hauling and dumping. Then she offered him a Coke. It was the least she could do.

He hung around with her outside on the patio for about an hour and when she went inside her phone was ringing.

"What happened?" Cindy asked in a hushed voice."Did the police actually come?"

"It was awful. The good news is I didn't get arrested. The bad news is the house was a wreck."

"Was?"

"Gabe helped me clean it up."

"I didn't see him at the party."

"I know, I didn't invite him."

"Then why . . . ?"

"Why did he help me? I don't know. He felt sorry for me, I guess. But he wasn't sorry for punching Steve in the face."

"What did he do that for? I missed all the fun."

"Tell you later. Right now I'm too tired."

"I feel awful. I'm the one who told you to have a party."

"I wanted to have one. But one was enough. From now on, no parties, no guys. I don't need them."

"Even Steve?"

"Especially Steve. I got a different impression of him tonight."

"Before or after he got punched?"

"Both. And starting tomorrow I'm no longer the rich bitch you used to know."

"You're rich but you're not a bitch."

"Okay, but I'm spoiled. There's always been somebody to clean up after me. Somebody who was paid to do it. Tonight somebody helped me just because he wanted to. Or because he felt sorry for me. I . . . I don't know. What I do know is that I'm not going to get pushed into doing something I don't want to do by some guy or my so-called big sister. I'm making my own decisions from now on."

"Good for you. See you Monday, Victoria. Don't forget it's Pet Day."

"Oh, no. I don't have a pet."

"I don't either. You can be my pet and I'll be yours."

Victoria drifted off to a restless sleep, hearing the sound of breaking glass in her dreams.

twenty-three

If your dog doesn't like someone, you probably shouldn't either.

—Golden Gate Fortune Cookies
(Fifteen Famous Flavors)

Though Victoria was hoping life would settle down and become simple now that her party was over, on Monday it got more complicated. And stranger.

She stumbled out of bed early to print out her paper on *A Tale of Two Cities.* Before she even had her makeup on or had combed her hair, there was a knock on the front door. With the paper in one hand, she grabbed a silk robe and ran to answer it. Through the peephole she saw it was Gabe with an enormous English sheepdog standing next to him, panting. The dog, not Gabe.

She opened the door and both Gabe and the dog stared at

her for a long moment without speaking. Okay, she probably looked awful, no makeup, hair standing on end, ink from her new printer cartridge on her fingers, but what did he expect at seven in the morning? What was he doing here anyway? And with a dog? Then it clicked: it was Pet Day at Manderley, the first day of National Pet Wellness Month. Hence the dog. But what did that have to do with her?

"What's wrong?" she said when Gabe continued to stand there gaping at her. Maybe he'd never seen a traditional red silk Chinese kimono with a hand-embroidered dragon design before. It was loose. It was comfortable. She tightened the sash.

He shifted his gaze away from the kimono to her face. "I need a ride to school."

"Fine, but it's too early. Can you just meet me by the car in a half an hour?"

"It's Dexter who needs a ride." He looked down at the dog. "He's going to school today."

"I didn't know you had a pet."

"I don't. He belongs to a friend of my mom's."

"You borrowed a dog for Pet Day?"

"No. Yes. Not me. *My* mom. At Parent Night one of my teachers told her I wasn't taking full advantage of the 'Manderley Experience,' whatever that is. So when she read about Pet

Day in the 'Manderley Weekly Online Memo for Parents,' she got me a pet for the day. I can't believe she did it without even telling me."

"I saw your mom that night. She was talking to one of your teachers, maybe the one who told her that."

"Who was it?"

"I don't know. It wasn't Mr. K or Julian." Why was he staring at her breasts like that? She tugged nervously at the red silk lapels. "Let me get this straight. You're asking me to give a dog a ride to school? In a gas-guzzler? Are you sure you want to subject this poor animal to gas fumes?" She couldn't help giving him a bad time after the lectures he'd given her. But she also threw in a little half smile so he'd know she wasn't really serious.

"Okay, I asked for that," he said. "It's not like I have a choice. The dog was brought over last night. Today my mom took her car into the shop for an oil change. So if you can't give him a ride, I'll just tie him up outside the house and you can forget I asked. Who cares about National Pet Wellness Month anyway? Not me and not Dexter."

She frowned. Was this the same guy who'd come to her rescue Friday night? Who had saved her from Steve? Who had called the taxis? Who'd hung around and talked about everything from astronomy to TV shows out on the patio where they had collapsed on deck chairs and stared up at the stars? Who'd acted like he thought she was a decent person, a nice person, even sometimes an interesting person, and was now acting like she was public enemy number one just because she was giving him a hard time? Like he hadn't done the same to her?

"I said I'd take him and I will," she said. "I owe you, you know that. For helping me after the party. You didn't have to do that." When she'd woken up the next morning, she'd realized he'd even hauled away the garbage cans and the pavement had been hosed off and washed clean.

He shrugged. "Forget it."

Victoria looked down at the dog. Dexter shook the hair out of his face, cocked his head and looked up at her with huge, sad eyes.

"You can't just tie up the dog. I don't mind giving him a ride. But you're coming too. For your sake I hope no one sees you riding with me. Your reputation would be in the toilet."

"What's that?" he said, gesturing down at her hand.

Victoria had almost forgotten about her ten-page paper.

" 'Themes of Guilt and Shame in *A Tale of Two Cities.*' "

"Can I read it? While I'm waiting for you?"

She hesitated. "I guess so. If you want to."

She handed it to him and closed the door. After all Gabe

had done for her the least she could do was give him and the dog a ride to school. Maybe Gabe had forgotten, but he'd told her they were going to start collecting DNA samples for his experiment today. She also had to turn in her paper. All that and Pet Day too.

She knew Gabe and his dog were waiting, but she needed some time to think before she could face the day. She perched at the breakfast bar where she sipped a cup of special yellow-gold oolong tea her parents had brought for her, opened the newspaper and read her horoscope. Not that she put any faith in it, but she needed something to take her mind off her problems.

" 'Don't feel guilty about asking for help. There's no shame in it. You will redeem yourself in the long run. Opposition comes from the moon/Saturn. Stay strong. Don't delay. Procrastination is your downfall.' "

How could she stay strong when she'd never been strong? She didn't feel strong. She felt guilty. Not for asking for help, just for having the party at all. She'd had it for all the wrong reasons. Redemption was what she'd attempted by spending two days doing homework and writing her paper and not even thinking about fashion, clothes, makeup or hair styles. Or trying not to, anyway.

When she was finally ready, Gabe was waiting for her by the car, glaring at it. At least he had the sense not to trash it verbally though. Instead he wanted to talk about her paper. She didn't. She had written it. It was done. She was handing it in today.

He sat there in the passenger seat tirelessly making suggestions on how to improve it. He was using words like *sacrifice*, *death* and *secrets* until her head hurt. "And by the way," he said, "you misspelled some words. Didn't you run spell-check?"

"I didn't have time. I just finished it. I know it's not perfect, but I don't care. I'm done and it's due today."

"Okay, whatever. It's your paper." He reached in the backseat and put the paper in her backpack. She drove slowly, the dog sitting behind her, breathing down her neck with his Alpo-laced breath.

"You really think I should say something about Carton's sacrifice and his final speech?" she asked when the silence got to her.

"It's pretty important."

"Uh-huh." She was not going to redo it. Even though she had a free period after lunch. Even though she had no pet to display today. It was clear Gabe had thought about the book. Of course he had; he'd read it before. He even liked it. He told her he'd discussed it in his class and written his own paper on it last year.

For the rest of the ride, he mercifully kept his mouth shut

about emissions, climate change or any of his other usual rants. Instead there was more silence. She just wondered where that close feeling she'd had with him Friday night had gone.

She should have known it wouldn't last. Not that she was lonely or that she needed him or anyone. For one night she thought it might be nice to have a guy friend. Different. Strange. But not bad.

She had no idea what Gabe did with Dexter after she let them out of the car. The whole campus was full of kids with pets, not just dogs and cats, but birds and snakes and hamsters in cages. Classes were interrupted by barking and hissing and scratching.

After a special Pet Wellness Month barbecue lunch out on the lawn, Victoria was surprised when Steve came up to her and asked her to hold on to his Labradoodle's leash while he took a break. Didn't he suffer one iota of shame about his behavior the other night? Apparently not.

He looked completely recovered from her party, except for a bruise on his chin. His eyes were clear and bluer than ever, so blue she felt like she could drown in them. His body was just as studly as ever. Every muscle still honed to perfection. But her heart did not flutter, not once. Her hands were steady, her knees sturdy. He didn't mention her party or his altercation with Gabe. Or even say why he needed to take a break. He just assumed she'd help him out.

And what did she do? Did she tell him she was busy, or that she didn't like dogs, or that she was mad at him for coming to her party drunk and refusing to leave when she asked him to? And for grabbing her when she didn't want to be grabbed?

No, she didn't. She was backpedaling like mad. When Steve flashed a smile at her, showing his perfect white teeth in his tanned face, she smiled back and said *yes.* She was a weakling. She reached for the leash and absently petted his dog.

"I thought you didn't have a dog," Cindy said when she saw Victoria a few minutes later.

"It's Steve's. I'm just dog-sitting for a minute."

"He'll never win the look-alike contest. It doesn't look at all like him," Cindy said. "You know who will? Your neighbor over there."

Victoria turned and saw Gabe with Dexter. Of course he would win. The hair in the face. She hadn't noticed earlier, but they both had the same matching expression on their faces that said, "I don't want to be here, but since I am, I'll take the prize." And they did.

twenty-four

You and me, friends Fur-Ever.

—Golden Gate Fortune Cookies
(Good luck, good taste too!)

Gabe didn't want to enter the contest and he really didn't want to win, but once he did, he wondered if maybe there was something to this "Manderley Experience" deal after all. Kids he didn't even know came up to him and asked to see his trophy. A couple of hot-looking girls and even some teachers, the headmaster and a few of the popular guys congratulated him. Girls said his dog was cute, but that he was even cuter. They leaned down to pet Dexter and talk to him in some kind of silly dog speak.

He had thought he was immune to flattery. He tried brushing it off when the girls said they could see how he won. Cute dog, cute owner. Truth was, this kind of thing had never happened at Castle.

He couldn't help it, his face turned red and he grinned stupidly in spite of himself. What was wrong with him, getting all impressed because some super-snobby girls were all over him with compliments? Was he getting mental or something? The only girl he was interested in was Victoria, and she only liked him because he helped her out at her party. He ought to give up on her—she was so not his type—but he wasn't ready to, not yet.

At first he thought she was just a pretty face. Pretty? She was beautiful, especially in that kimono thing this morning, or jeans or a skirt, with paint on her face, whatever. Then after they talked the night of the party he realized there was something more to her than her looks. A lot. Her ideas, her background made her frigging irresistible, and that wasn't good. They were so different, way, way too different.

A couple of girls asked if they could take his dog for a walk. He said sure. Why not? All the chaos today might give him the chance he needed to collect some samples for his experiment without anyone noticing.

Victoria was holding the leash of a weird-looking hybrid dog.

"What's that?" he asked, frowning.

"A Labradoodle. I don't know his name but he belongs to . . . someone."

"Give him back. Now is a good time to collect samples."

"How is it good, it's the middle of Pet Day?"

"Because everyone's distracted. We go around snatching drinking glasses or cutting off chunks of hair and no one will notice. I don't necessarily want anyone to know what I'm doing."

"Why not?"

"People are funny about their DNA. They might wonder why I want it."

"Why do you?"

"To see if I can get any matches."

"I don't get it. Isn't this an expensive test?"

"Mr. K says it's within the science budget, so don't worry about it. You don't have to pay for it, and neither do I. You just have to help me."

"I've got this dog here," Victoria protested. "I can't just dump him, he's not mine."

A few minutes later the dog took matters into his own hands, er, paws. Victoria got rid of her dog, or rather her dog got rid of her. It bolted, jerking the leash out of her hand. It ran through the crowds on the lawn, kicking up its heels and knocking over a table with dog food in small sample envelopes and pamphlets on pet care.

Victoria screamed. Like a moron, Gabe responded as if he'd heard a cry for help and ran after the dog. The stupid dog that wasn't even hers. He ran past groups of giggling girls who turned to look as he went by, past couples sitting on the senior bench who paid no attention to him, and past stoners coming from the parking lot who gave him glazed puzzled looks. Finally he caught the dog as it ran out through the brick entrance under the hand-carved "Manderley Prepratory School; Founded 1915" sign.

When he brought the dog back Victoria thanked him with a big smile. She had the most amazing smile, the kind you didn't expect and that caught you off-guard. What was wrong with him? He'd fallen for her the first day of school and it just kept getting worse.

No matter what she said or what she did he just couldn't shake off his attraction to her, the last girl in the world he should go after. The poorest guy in the whole school was drooling over the richest girl. What was the point? There was none.

When Victoria handed over the dog to its owner and that owner happened to be Steve, the jerk who'd attacked her the night of her party, he really felt like an idiot. Why hadn't he just let the stupid dog go?

And when Steve complained that Victoria had screwed

up, Gabe thought about punching him out again. If he'd had another bucket of water he would have gladly dumped it on Steve's head.

The guy didn't seem to recognize Gabe. So what if he did? Gabe wasn't afraid of a big macho sports star, sober or drunk.

"Wait a minute," Gabe said. "She didn't *let* him go; he went."

Steve turned and glared at him as if he'd just dropped out of the sky to annoy him. "Who asked you, asshole?" he said.

"Nobody. What's wrong with you? Your dog is as big a dick as you are."

"Wait, I know you who are," Steve said, rubbing his chin where Gabe had decked him.

"Yeah, I know who you are too. You're the drunk scumbag who got hauled away from the party."

"You wouldn't have hit me if I had been sober."

"Well, if you're ever sober enough, let me know and I'll try again."

"Payback's a bitch," Steve said, his lip curled.

"Just try it," Gabe said.

Steve stalked away without trying it or thanking either of them for saving his dog.

"Sorry about that," Victoria said. "I think the dog took off because all the other dogs were running around too."

"Mob mentality," Gabe muttered. "That's what we call it."

Victoria looked at him with something that might have been respect, or maybe she was just annoyed. Then, as if they'd agreed on it, they both pretended the confrontation with Steve hadn't happened.

"Like in *A Tale of Two Cities*," she said slowly. "Mob mentality is what happened during the revolution, isn't it?"

"Yeah, like that. You sure you don't want to rewrite your paper?"

She looked at her watch. "I thought we were going to collect DNA samples."

"Right," he said. He understood her now. Sometimes it was easier to work on someone else's project than your own. For him his DNA thing was more important than some paper for Brit Lit. After all, it might tell him who he was. But why should she help him when she had other things to do?

It didn't look like she was doing anything at all at the moment except standing there staring off in space. Maybe she was still thinking about Steve. He was the type girls liked. Maybe he didn't look like his dog, but he sure acted like him: thoughtless, impulsive, brainless. Only the dog couldn't help it. Steve could.

Was that really what girls liked? It didn't matter. He wasn't going to get into that mess again. Not after what happened with Natalie at Castle last year. The girl had ripped his heart out and thrown it away. He'd thought she was the one. He told her everything, how he missed having a dad, how he put his feelings into his art. He even painted a picture for her. She didn't get it. She just made a joke about it.

He'd learned a lot from her: Hold back. Don't let your feelings show. Don't tell girls anything because they'll use it against you. He'd done all the wrong things and she'd thrown them back in his face. She wasn't rich and spoiled like certain Manderley girls. But she had been trouble all the same. He would never go there again.

twenty-five

You will soon be more aware of your growing awareness.

—Golden Gate Fortune Cookies
(A cookie a day keeps the doctor away)

"I've got rubber gloves for us, scissors and plastic bags for the samples," Gabe said.

"Samples of what?" Victoria asked. "And don't say DNA. I know that. How are we getting samples of DNA and who are we getting them from?"

"Teachers, we're getting them from teachers. We're cutting pieces of their hair or we're getting saliva. I told you."

She stumbled over a fallen branch on the grass and almost fell. Automatically Gabe caught her by the arm. She shot a surprised look in his direction. What did she think, that he'd let her trip and fall?

"Over there." He nudged her with his elbow. "See that picnic table under the tree with those teachers sitting at it?"

"Yes. So?"

"We say we're on the Pet Wellness Month Cleanup Committee and ask if we can clear their table. Then we grab their water bottles or paper cups or whatever has saliva on it."

"What's the big mystery? Why don't we just say we're collecting DNA samples for our chem experiment? Then we'll be able to match their names with the samples, or isn't that important?"

"Yeah, of course, but some people might not want their DNA tested," he said.

"Why, because they're criminals, they've got some kind of record?"

"I don't know. People are funny. Everyone's got secrets. Don't you?"

"Yes, but nothing I'm going to learn from my DNA. I know who I am. I've got my mother's looks but unfortunately not my father's brain."

They paused under an oak tree and watched the teachers who were watching the pet parade. "This DNA thing is about you, isn't it?" she asked.

"I know who I am, but I don't know who my dad is," he blurted out. Might as well tell her because as his partner she'd probably find out anyway. Yeah, he wasn't going to trust anyone, especially another girl, but just this once . . . What harm could it do?

"Really? And you think he's one of the teachers?" she asked. "Why?"

Her clear hazel eyes were wide with surprise. Just like they had been this morning when she'd opened the door in that red robe she'd been wearing, looking so hot he couldn't catch his breath. The funny thing was, the more he knew her, the more he wanted her, and not just for that cool/hot body of hers, but for her brain too, and for the way she talked.

She was the most exotic girl he'd ever met. He was trying, but he couldn't get the picture of her in her robe out of his mind. It had kept slipping to give him a glimpse of skin. He'd wanted to see more. Much more.

"Why?" He jerked his brain back to the subject. "Because my mom acted all weird when I asked if my dad was a teacher. Then she clammed up. Typical. That's what she always does. You know how much your family pays her. No way she can afford to send me here unless my dad is on the faculty, because teachers' kids get a free ride."

"Maybe you've got a scholarship."

He snorted. "Because I'm so smart?"

"Aren't you?

"No."

"Your artistic ability?"

He laughed. It sounded strange to his ears. He hadn't laughed once since he'd started at Manderley. He felt the skin around his mouth stretch tight. He hoped his lips wouldn't crack.

"I'm serious," she said. "I think you're good."

Second time she'd said that. Maybe she meant it. "Yeah? Well, I did enter that mural contest, so we'll see if anyone else thinks I'm any good. And I had nothing else to do, so . . ."

"What? No more fun experiments with floating bubbles or measuring the pH of pond scum or . . ."

"No more."

"And don't forget the garage wall."

"Uh-huh," he said. "Okay, let's do this. We'll split up. You take that table over there. Try it your way. I'll go to the cafeteria and see who's there."

"What about Dexter? Maybe you could use him for a decoy or a distraction."

Why hadn't he thought of that? "He's gone, but that's not a bad idea."

She raised one arched eyebrow. "Two compliments in one day. You're getting soft, Thomas."

He wasn't sure if she was annoyed, amused or pleased. He

thought he'd had her pegged. But he was wrong, There was more to her than just those exotic good looks. He didn't have a chance with her, he knew that, but who didn't want what he couldn't have? Especially a girl who's smart, fun and beautiful too.

Right now all he wanted was to find out who his father was. He meant what he said. Using the dog was a good idea. If he could find him before lunch was over and all the cups and glasses with the tell-tale saliva were gone . . .

She was staring at him.

"What? What's wrong? Do I have mustard on my face?"

"I just wondered, have you seen that new spy movie?"

"No, why, are you asking me on a date?"

"No! Somebody said you look like the guy who plays the hero, except for your hair."

"You're just trying to get me to cut it."

She shrugged and he took off to sneak around and pick up plastic cups from the table where the faculty members were eating, but he didn't know whose was whose. It didn't matter. If he found one match he'd know his father was there at Manderley and that would explain everything—his mother's determination to get him into this school and how she'd managed it without tuition money. It would be a big step forward. Today he knew nothing, but when he got the results back from the lab, he might know something.

twenty-six

Avoid combustible materials for the next twenty-four hours.

—Golden Gate Fortune Cookies
(Available in seven delicious flavors)

"Not bad," Gabe said when Victoria handed him four paper cups with names on them and five hair clippings, also with names.

"Not bad? I got more than you did. And I told the truth. Oh, not about your lack of, uh, male parentage," she said. "I told them I was doing a chem experiment. I know you thought it was a lame idea, but I did it anyway. They don't know me and they don't know you, so what's the harm?" She carefully put the samples into the drawer under their table in the lab.

Before he could answer, three junior girls she didn't know, dressed more or less alike in denim miniskirts, tunics and clunky sandals, came into the lab with his dog. Didn't they have any sense of individuality?

"Hey, Gabe." The girl sidled up to him like they were old friends. Good old friends.

"There you are," another said.

"We've been looking for you."

He grinned at them. He looked downright pleased to see them. He'd never grinned at her. Or looked that pleased to see her. And she'd just done over half of his experiment for him. Maybe he was grinning at his dog. Pleased to see him again. Sure, that was it.

"Your dog is so cute," one girl said, shoving Victoria aside with a sharp elbow to the ribs as she came up to the lab table.

Victoria opened her mouth to protest, but nothing came out.

"Yeah, we just love him," said another, reaching down to pet the dog.

"He's cute, isn't he?" Victoria said. It was time they all realized she was alive and well and not some cardboard cutout to be pushed aside. The first girl, the one who was sticking to Gabe like rubber cement, turned and gave her a coolly dismissive glance. The two others turned their backs to her as if she didn't count. No doubt hoping she'd disappear.

"Can we keep him for a while?"

"I guess. If you want. He's not even mine," Gabe said.

"What if we enter him in the race?"

"There's a race? Okay, sure. I'd better come with you though."

"Wait," Victoria said, but no one heard her.

She stood in the middle of the lab watching the three girls, Gabe and the dog walk out as if she'd expired in a puff of noxious chemical fumes. No more important than if she was part of the lab equipment. She didn't expect anything from the snotty girls, but Gabe hadn't even thanked her, had he?

Okay, he was gone, so now what? How long was Pet Day going to be? Personally she'd had enough pets for today. She'd had enough sample collecting too. It was time for some "Victoria time."

She went to the computer lab and brought her paper on *A Tale of Two Cities* up on the screen. While reading it over she thought about what Gabe had said. She knew she'd left a lot out. She knew she had to give examples of sacrifice, death and secrets. She knew she had to tell the meaning of Carton's sacrifice. But she didn't know how and it taxed her brain to think so much.

All she really wanted to do was draw pictures of clothes. She had an idea for a coat with narrow lapels, hardly any lapels at all, very narrow . . . And a gown . . . It would only take a few minutes.

But the words of her horoscope came rushing back. *Don't delay. Procrastination is your downfall.*

It took her the rest of the afternoon to get her head around her paper. She missed a few classes, but she finished just in time for English, her last period. Breathlessly she climbed the wide staircase to the second floor of the Gertrude Manderley Mansion to find a note on the blackboard.

"In honor of our pets, British Lit is canceled today. Papers due tomorrow."

Victoria stood in the deserted room staring at the board, her paper in hand. So all that rush had been for nothing. She could have written her paper tonight and had time to spell-check it too and then handed it in tomorrow. If only she hadn't read that stupid horoscope that gave her faulty advice.

"Victoria."

It was Steve, with his hair damp, his T-shirt stuck to his sweaty chest, and his dog on the end of his leash. Come to think of it, they did look something alike. Curly hair, wide-set eyes, tongue hanging out.

"Glad I caught you. Want to apologize for that misunderstanding the other night. Really had a great time at your party."

"Good," she said, but she didn't really believe him. How could he consider being punched and hauled away in a taxi a great time?

"Class is canceled," she said. As if he couldn't read for himself.

"Lucky break. I bet half the class didn't have their papers done." He shaded his eyes from the late afternoon sun that slanted through the high windows. "Did you?"

"Just finished it," she said, holding it up. "But who knows if it's any good. I had a hard time with the book."

"I hear you. It was a real bitch. In fact I'm still working on it. How many pages is yours?"

Victoria thumbed through her report. "About ten I guess. It might be ten pages of crap. Who knows?"

"I'll let you in on my secret. First, tell them what you're going to say, then say it, then tell them what you said."

"That sounds simple."

"It is. I'll be glad to check it over for you, if you want."

"Oh, well . . ." Reluctantly she handed it to him. She had no idea if Steve was a good writer or not. He never said much in class, but some smart kids didn't. "I know there're mistakes. I didn't have time to check my spelling for one thing . . ."

"I'll do it. Don't worry. You know, I really miss our Chinese sessions," he said, sliding her paper into his binder. "I had to drop it this semester."

"That's too bad. You were doing really well."

"Come on, was I really?" he said with the grin she used

to find so irresistible. Now it seemed forced and kind of irritating.

"Steve?" It was a guy in a Manderley Water Polo shirt standing in the doorway. "Let's go."

"Coming." He looked at Victoria. "I'll bring your paper to you tomorrow."

"If I don't see you, I can print out another copy. Since it's not due till class tomorrow I might look it over again."

He nodded and walked past her and out the door, while she stood there listening to his footsteps fade away.

twenty-seven

If the ring finger is longer than the index finger, you are likely to be successful. Or not.

—Golden Gate Fortune Cookies
(From all natural ingredients)

Who knew DNA testing would be such a hot topic? When Mr. K told the class about Victoria and Gabe's experiment all the students wanted to be tested. Sure, it was an expensive test, but hey, this was Manderley, where expense was not an issue. Not with their healthy endowment, thanks to wealthy alums. If they could afford a new tennis complex with lighted courts, an all-natural food court and a recording studio for the jazz band, why couldn't every kid run a DNA test on himself and his dog or whoever else they wanted to be related to?

Some kids thought maybe they'd been switched at birth, others thought they couldn't be related to a certain older brother, bitchy sister, controlling father, mother, whatever. Kids were bringing in hair samples to add to the stack to be sent to the lab. Others wanted to exhume bodies from graves, but Mr. K. drew the line there.

In class everyone lined up so Gabe and Victoria could take swabs of mucus from the inside of their mouths or cut a piece of their hair. Some people murmured "gross," but Victoria and Gabe swabbed their mucus anyway. They put the samples in plastic bags, labeled them and put everything in a big envelope along with the samples they'd collected on Pet Day and addressed it to the DNA testing lab in Sacramento.

"Hey, I didn't get a sample of your hair," Gabe said to Victoria after class, scissors in hand.

"I told you I know who I am but whatever, go ahead," she said.

He leaned forward and carefully cut a few strands. His face was so close to hers she could see that he hadn't shaved. She had a funny urge to run her finger along his jaw to see how rough it felt. She clenched her fingers together to keep from giving in to her crazy impulse.

"You're next," she said.

He backed away as if he was afraid to get too close to her. "I already did mine."

She surveyed his hair with narrowed eyes, trying to imagine

what he'd look like without that mop hanging in his face. "You said I could cut your hair."

"Uh . . ." he said. "Where?"

"Here looks good."

"Oh, why not? Get it over with."

"Okay." She reached into her purse and pulled out a small leather case.

"You bring your scissors to school?"

"They're not scissors. They're professional shears, handmade in Japan. I never go anywhere without them." She turned and put her hands on his shoulders. "Sit down."

Then she went to get the trash can from the corner of the room and a plastic sheet that had been used for a defunct experiment using Gro-Lights and dwarf plants.

"You're serious about this, aren't you?" he asked.

She nodded and lifted a chunk of his hair. It was soft and thick and smelled clean and musky at the same time. She snipped, she shaped, she trimmed and cut it in layers.

Finally she stepped back and studied his face. She tried to be objective, but she couldn't. He looked that much better. He looked older, tougher, sexier. She'd always wanted to do this. She loved doing makeovers. But this time she'd gone too far. She made him look too old, too tough and *way* too sexy. What had she done? Now she wanted to bury her face in his hair.

Then put her hands on his shoulders and . . . What was she thinking? That wasn't part of the deal.

"Done?" he asked.

"Uh-huh."

What if he didn't like it? What if he felt like she'd gone too far, cut too much? Didn't matter. She'd done a great job. Someone would appreciate it, his mother for one, and probably about half the girls at Manderley. Including herself.

She pulled a tiny compact out of her bag, flipped it open and handed it to him. "What do you think?"

He looked in the mirror with narrowed eyes. Finally his mouth turned up at the corners and he looked at her. Without all that hair he looked stripped to the bone, sexy, rugged and almost vulnerable too.

"What do *you* think?" he asked.

"I like it," she said. Now *that* was the understatement of the year.

twenty-eight

If you're going through hell, keep going.

—Golden Gate Fortune Cookies
(Like nothing you've ever tasted)

"Where are you going?" Gabe's mother asked.

He grabbed his leather jacket. "Out."

Actually he didn't know where he was going. He knew where he wanted to go—right over to the big house, knock on the door, walk in, and say hey. But there was a car in the driveway. Victoria had company.

So he walked around her house instead, through the damp grass, the collar of his jacket up against his bare neck, glancing in at the rooms that looked like they belonged in *Architectural Digest*. Of course he didn't read *Architectural Digest*, but this had to be what the houses they featured looked like. He was used to living above the garage of those houses or in the caretaker's cottage, but he hardly ever went inside the big house.

He'd been in the kitchen the night of the party, but that's all. He probably shouldn't go anywhere near there tonight. She hadn't invited him. Maybe she was having another party.

He found her room and stopped outside on the patio on the other side of the sliding glass doors. She was there with two other girls, the redhead and the one he recognized from chem lab. All were wearing oversized men's shirts smeared with paint. They were working on a project.

Her room was a replica of the Sleeping Beauty Castle at Disneyland, his mom's favorite place that she'd dragged him to every year on her birthday until he said he was too old for Mr. Frog's Ride and begged her to stop. Victoria's bed had four tall posts and was covered in something that looked like mosquito netting. God forbid she should be attacked by bugs.

He stood behind a fir tree where they couldn't see him and watched the girls like they were on a TV. That's how different the scene was from anything in his world. Three rich girls. No, wait, the redhead said she had a scholarship. But still.

Victoria's bedroom seemed to be equipped with everything. A Media Center PC, a big carousel of CDs, speakers for surround-sound in every corner, a huge plasma TV mounted on the wall, a walk-in closet and an elliptical trainer. The place reeked of money and privilege. No wonder she acted like she was different from him and everybody else. She was.

He moved closer to try to hear what they were saying. They couldn't possibly see him, and what if they could? He'd say he was out for a walk. Or that he was looking for the back door to knock and ask to borrow something his mom needed. What was the big deal? Their voices were muffled, but maybe if he got a little closer he'd be able to see whose picture was on that big poster. Holy shit. Was that Victoria in a bra? He had to get a better look at that.

twenty-nine

Forget injury, never forget kindness.

—Golden Gate Fortune Cookies
(Surprise your guests with good fortune)

"Tell me again why I'm doing this, Cindy," Victoria said, setting a big poster board that read "Show Me the Money—Vote for Victoria" on an easel to dry.

"Power, popularity and because you got nominated by your big sister who wants what's best for you," Cindy said.

"You haven't seen the latest," Victoria said. "Look what she's done now." She pointed to a giant poster of herself in a Victoria's Secret hip-hugger and push-up bra with the caption "Victoria's Real Secret—She's Our Next Treasurer." "Ta da!"

Maggie and Cindy screamed in unison.

"Is that you?" Cindy demanded.

"Of course it's not me." She lifted her shirt and flashed her small breasts at them. She giggled. "Oh, the face is me, as you can see, but the body is so *not* me."

"But where did you get it?" Maggie asked.

"Brooke had it made at Kinko's after she didn't like the ones I had made. She thinks it's fabulous. I almost passed out when I saw it. You don't know my mother, but if she saw this . . . she'd do more than pass out."

"Wait, I thought you were in beauty contests back in Hong Kong," Cindy said.

"Miss Junior Hong Kong, yes, but we did *not* appear in our underwear. Ever."

"What are you going to do with it?" Maggie asked.

"Burn it. Toss it in the trash. I don't know. I'll tell you what I'm not doing with it—posting it at school. I don't want to be treasurer that bad. I don't want to be treasurer at all."

"So for something a little more subdued . . ." Maggie said, holding up a poster board with "Put Your Money Where My Math Is" written on it and a big picture of a pair of lips.

"Sweet," Cindy said with a big smile. "Have you got some more Magic Markers?"

"Let me look." Victoria crossed the room to the dresser where she kept her art supplies. After she opened the door to one of the high cabinets, she stood on her toes and riffled through stacks of paper, tubes of acrylic paint, colored pencils, charcoal, ink and pens, but found nothing.

Then she opened the lower cabinet and pushed aside a pile of cashmere sweaters her mother had insisted on buying.

"I have a whole new box here somewhere . . ." At that instant she saw something reflected in the mirror on the dresser—a man was standing outside on the patio. A pale face with dark eyes staring in at her. "*Arrgh!*" she blurted. Her head jerked up and cracked against the still-open cabinet door. She crumpled to the floor.

A minute later, or maybe it was longer . . . the story of Rip Van Winkle came to her confused mind . . . she came to. She had no idea if she'd been unconscious for days, weeks, maybe years? Maybe the election was over and she'd defaulted. That would be a relief.

Maybe high school was over and she was still in a coma. Now maybe they'd let her go to design school when she woke up. If she could still draw. Maybe she'd be even better. There'd be a whole new season, new designers, new ideas. Surely it would be too late to take the SATs and go to Berkeley.

Her head was pounding, and the voices she heard seemed to come from far away. They called her name but she couldn't answer. She wanted to tell them not to pull the plug on her. She was fine. But was she? Her mouth was too dry to speak.

She tried to sit up but her head felt so heavy she couldn't lift it.

"What happened?" Maggie asked, her forehead creased with worry lines. She and Cindy were kneeling on the floor next to Victoria.

Her hands shaking, Victoria pointed to the glass doors. "Sssssomebody out there."

Cindy jumped up and pressed her nose against the glass. "It's him, your neighbor. Should I let him in?"

"Oh, uh . . . sure." Gabe. That's who was outside looking in at her. But why? What did he want?

When Cindy opened the sliding glass door to the patio a rush of fresh air came in with him that helped clear her brain. He leaned over her. His face was so different without all the hair in his eyes that she almost didn't recognize him. The way he loomed over her in his leather jacket made him look bigger and rougher than she remembered.

"Sorry I scared you," he said. "You're getting a lump on your head. You should put some ice on it."

"In the kitchen," Victoria said, still groggy.

"I'll get it," Maggie said.

Cindy looked up at Gabe and then down at Victoria. "I'll go with her. Will you be all right?" she asked, wedging a frilly little pillow under Victoria's head.

" 'Course. I'm fine, really," she said lifting her head to see if she could. "Just a little groggy. Oh, while you're in the kitchen? Bring some drinks and the stuff on the counter." Her mother, the consummate hostess, would be proud of her. For once. Even lying on the floor, suffering from a knock on the head, she was thinking of her guests.

If only they'd all forget that she'd freaked out just because her neighbor was outside on the patio. Gabe must think she was even more of a wimp than he had before. Not much she could do about that, just try to act normal for the rest of the evening.

He kneeled down on the carpet and held up two fingers.

"How many?"

"Three," she said. She had to do something to lighten the mood, to show she wasn't a complete wuss. He frowned. "Just kidding. Two fingers. I know what you're doing. You think I have a concussion. I don't. Really. I'm fine. What were you doing out there anyway?"

"Me? I came over to borrow something. I knocked on the door but you didn't hear me so I walked around until I heard you and . . . Sorry, I didn't mean to scare you."

"Well you did." She rubbed her head. "Why didn't you call first?"

"I didn't have your number."

Victoria frowned. He had her number. At least, his mother

did. And if he wanted to borrow something, what was it? He wasn't making any sense, but she blamed her fuzzy brain and not him. The smell of his leather jacket and the fresh air he brought in with him made her feel better.

"Isn't the next question supposed to be who's president?" she asked. "To make sure I'm conscious and my memory is okay?"

He looked around the room at the posters propped against the wall. "Whoever's president, looks like you're gonna be treasurer. With a poster like that who wouldn't vote for you?"

She blushed. No doubt which one he meant. Too bad she hadn't burned it yet. "That's not me." She lifted her head for another look at it.

"Yeah? Looks like you," he said.

"From the neck up, yes. But the body? In my dreams."

"Nothing wrong with your body," he muttered. "But a treasurer only needs a brain, right?"

"Which is why I'm not using that poster."

"You sure? You might get a lot of votes."

"You think I won't win unless I use it?"

"I didn't mean that. I like your real body better. What I've seen of it anyway."

"Wait. How long were you out there?"

"Me? Just a few minutes. Why?" he said innocently.

He might say no, but the look on his face told her he'd seen her baring her breasts. She felt a relapse coming on. Her face was hot, her head was spinning. It was either the knock on the head or the unexpected compliment from Gabe or the thought that he really had seen her. She closed her eyes. "Unless I get more brain function I am not running for treasurer," she said.

"What's this about not running?" Cindy asked. She handed the bag of ice wrapped in a towel to Gabe, who set it gently on Victoria's head. Maggie was carrying a tray with nuts and chips and cans of soda and mineral water.

"Don't even think about backing out," Cindy said. "Not after we've made all these signs. You're going to win and you're going to be a great treasurer. Won't she?"

"Sure," Gabe said.

"Sure," Maggie echoed. She looked at Gabe. "Hey, you cut your hair."

"Looks great," Cindy said, beaming at him.

He looked pleased but embarrassed. Then he got to his feet and looked at the sliding glass doors he'd come through. "I should be going," he said.

"No, wait," Victoria said, pressing the ice bag against her head. "Stay. Have something to drink. We need your help. Gabe can draw," she told her friends. "He's good. He's going to win the library's mural contest."

"Cool," Cindy said. "Here's a paintbrush. I was going for a calligraphy look, you know what I mean?"

While the others—including Gabe—got involved working on her posters, Victoria quietly got up and turned on her CD player.

Hong Kong pop music was not that different from American pop music. Her new friends were not that different from her old friends. They gossiped, they ate, they laughed and they helped each other. Except her new friends were here and the others weren't. A warm fuzzy feeling crept up on her that might have been the result of the bump on her head, or not. She didn't want to be treasurer, but running for treasurer was turning out to be better than she thought.

thirty

You win some, you lose some.

—Golden Gate Fortune Cookies
(Because that's the way the cookie crumbles)

"Found out who's running against you," Brooke said when she saw her on campus a few days later. "Steve Heller."

"Oh, no." Victoria's heart sank.

"What's wrong? Who's going to vote for a jock for treasurer?" Brooke asked.

"Everyone. He's not only a jock, he's popular too."

"Remember what I told you, Vicky, the majority of the kids in your class are unpopular. That's your base. That's who you have to win over. So be friendly."

"I am friendly." But was she really? Was she going up to strangers and introducing herself and handing out fortune cookies? No, she wasn't. She might make an okay treasurer if she had the family accountant help her, but she'd never be a good politician.

"Surprise! I made campaign buttons for you," Brooke said. She held out a bright pink round button with the picture of Victoria in her push-up bra and hip-hugger panties. The button had "Victoria's Secret for Treasurer" written on it. It was embarrassing, disgusting, and it didn't even make sense. The only good thing was that it was so small it was hard to see unless you got up close.

"Brooke, I can't hand these out. First, it makes me look trashy, and second, it's not me. Not the body anyway."

"Of course it's you. Everyone will recognize you. Come on, Vicky, do you want to win or not?"

"Yes, but . . . I've got the cookies to hand out."

"Sure, hand out the cookies, but the buttons are what's going to get attention."

"That's what I'm afraid of," Victoria muttered.

Brooke just shrugged, left a bag of buttons for Victoria, kept one for herself and went off to hand them out. There was nothing Victoria could do to stop her without sounding like she'd already given up and didn't want to win.

It was too late to back out of the race now. Not with hundreds of fortune cookies, posters and buttons already made.

Cindy had rented the helium tank to blow up balloons. Fortunately the big poster of Victoria half naked was carefully hidden under her bed at home. It was bad enough that Gabe had seen it and compared her real body to the one in the picture. She still didn't know for sure if he'd actually seen her when she'd exposed herself that night. She couldn't think about it without feeling like a slut.

The campus was humming early Monday morning, or rather pounding with the sound of music coming from loud speakers, and political signs were everywhere. The headmaster had mercifully limited the campaigning to one day, and Victoria was really grateful. She was tired of the campaign and it hadn't even really started. Cindy had enlisted Marco to help put up the signs, and even Gabe showed up on his bike. Now if only she could avoid running into Steve.

"Sure you don't object to the helium balloons?" she asked Gabe when he offered to help her tie blue balloons with "Victoria" written on them in gold to the portico of the Gertrude Manderley Mansion. He was on the top of the ladder, she was at the bottom looking up. "I know how you feel about pollution," she said.

"Helium is an inert gas."

"Oh, right," she said. "But what about when the balloons get loose and go floating up into the air?"

He looked down at her, his mouth quirked in a reluctant half smile. She had to admit that he was more attractive than she'd first thought. Much more. Especially without the hair in his face. But it was more than that. It was his attitude. He'd actually smiled a few times. He'd changed. Or maybe she had.

Certain other girls seemed to think he was hot too. Her friends, for instance, and those girls who wanted to walk his dog for him. And that was before the haircut. Now he must be fighting them off. Or not fighting them off at all.

"I think the damage to the atmosphere will be minimal," he said.

She was still surprised he'd stayed so late at her house on Friday night. After the girls left, he was still there working on posters using calligraphy to write "If You Want the Best—Vote for Victoria for Junior Class Treasurer" on each one.

"How come you can do such nice calligraphy and I can't?" she'd asked, admiring his work.

"I'm an artist. You said so yourself. By the way, I've started on the garage wall."

"Can I see it?

"Not till I'm done."

It was true, he was a real artist, no matter what Julian thought. The small abstract painting his mother had hung on the kitchen wall was striking. If he was half that good at painting murals, he'd win the contest.

She knew Gabe had always thought she was a dullard, lacking in basic scientific knowledge, artistic talent or an ability to understand the themes in *A Tale of Two Cities*. Had he changed his mind after staying late at her house talking about those same things? She hoped so.

He'd asked her to tell him about Hong Kong and she tried to explain what living there was like. "It's different, but it's not another planet."

She and Gabe had talked and ate the snacks and later she brewed a pot of green tea.

"It's called Bird's Tongue tea because of all the tender new shoots," she had said as she poured it into two cups from a yellow and red porcelain pot. "Very labor-intensive to pick."

The tea had been soothing and stimulating at the same time as green tea is supposed to be. He had said he liked it. He drank two cups and he hadn't left until some time after midnight.

"Thanks for helping me," she had said at the front door. "Again. This is getting to be a habit. You showing up and bailing me out of something, I mean." She'd realized she liked it when he showed up. She liked their late-night conversations when it felt like they were the only two people in the world still awake.

"My fault you hit your head. I'm sorry about that. Blame the poster. I had to have a closer look." He had grinned and put his cool hand on her head. "How do you feel?"

She had meant to say she was fine, but nothing came out of her mouth. The touch of his hand, and the cool night air had made her shiver. He'd kissed her on the cheek, then he'd turned and gone home to his house above her garage.

She'd stood on the doorstep staring into the darkness. Had he really kissed her on the cheek or was she hallucinating? Had he just seen the poster of her or more? She might have been fine, but she'd been anything but normal. It must have been that bump on her head. Couldn't have been the kiss. If it had been real, it was nothing. Just a brush of his cool lips against her warm cheek. Just an afterthought. So why couldn't she forget it?

She'd fallen asleep wondering if she'd been in a coma all evening and hadn't really understood what was happening at all. That's how bizarre it had been.

thirty-one

Avoid taking unnecessary gambles.

—Golden Gate Fortune Cookies
(With a deep, inviting aroma)

"How come you didn't tell me you were running for treasurer?" Steve asked.

Victoria almost fell off her stepladder while she was taping a poster to a tree. Not the sexy poster, but another one that didn't make her look like she belonged on *Baywatch*.

Steve had never looked better or more surprised than he did now in his Manderley Water Polo shirt, baggy shorts and year-round tan. His eyes were wide open and as blue as the Manderley olympic pool water. No way could he have stayed up late last night making posters or stuffing fortunes into cookies. He probably had his many friends do it for him.

"I don't know. You didn't ask," she said.

That morning Victoria admired Steve as she would a male model. Her heart didn't skip a beat. Not a goose bump on her arms. This was the guy she had wanted to like her. This was the guy she had thought she was in lust with. No longer. What had happened to her?

Whatever it was it had happened before she hit her head. She hadn't felt the same about him for a long time. Any yet on Friday night something got knocked askew in her brain. The rest of the weekend had been hazy. Would she ever be the same again? Did she want to be? Even though Steve didn't make her skin tingle all over or make her heart race the way it used to, she knew if she hadn't been running for office, she'd still vote for him. She might vote for him anyway.

"Hey, here's your paper." He reached into his backpack and handed it to her. "Sorry I'm late with it. But you printed out another one, right? I didn't even get a chance to read it. Too much going on."

"For sure," she said. Only a loser would admit they didn't have too much going on.

"You'll probably win the election. A hot-looking girl for treasurer? That's a slam dunk."

"Oh no, you're going to win. Everyone knows you from basketball. I'm new here."

"What are you gonna say in your speech today?" he asked.

"Uh . . ." The old Victoria would have told him. She would have reached into her backpack and handed her speech to him to read. Something told her not to.

"Don't tell me," he said. "I know. First you're gonna tell them what you're gonna tell them, then you're gonna tell them, then you're gonna tell them what you told them, am I right?"

Victoria smiled politely. Her cool Miss Junior Hong Kong smile.

He reached out and gave her a handful of M&M's with his name on each one in tiny letters. "May the best person win," he said.

thirty-two

Tell the truth, that way you don't have to remember what you said.

—Golden Gate Fortune Cookies
(Whatever your mood, there's a cookie for you)

The gym was packed, balloons floated to the ceiling, some with Victoria's name on them. The school jazz band played out of tune, as usual. Even Cindy, the best clarinet player they had, admitted they weren't in top form these days. The popular senior girls sat together in the back row looking bored and blasé, the nerds sat together on one side and the jocks on the other. The rest of the gym was full of the vast majority—the unpopular ones—which was exactly where Victoria belonged.

Not today. Today she sat on the elevated rafter next to Brooke, who'd written Victoria's speech for her. Her hands were ice cold and her head was spinning. She'd never spoken to a large group before. She'd never spoken to a small group, for that matter.

She glanced to her left and saw Steve holding his speech in his steady hands, oozing self confidence while she was wondering if she'd be able to speak at all.

But she did. She told the entire student body, the popular and the unpopular, the teachers and the headmaster, how because she was an outsider she was able to see what needed to be done.

"I'm dedicated to new ideas," she read, though she had no idea what those would be. Her speech was mostly vague, about how she would reform the current fiscal situation at Manderley. Though she did mention how much better the dances would be, along with the transportation and uniforms for the sports teams *if* they voted for her.

When she finished speaking, there was polite applause while she tossed handfuls of fortune cookies into the crowd, then she sat down.

Steve's speech was even shorter than hers and was interrupted by his friends standing and throwing M&M's into the crowd. The kids yelled, cheered and stamped their feet on the polished floor of the gym.

"I hope you handed out all of those buttons I had made," Brooke said, as they walked out of the gym together. "Let's go vote."

Of course Brooke couldn't vote for her, because she was a senior. Not that one vote mattered. Victoria knew she'd lose; she'd always known it. She'd even wanted to lose. So why did she feel so depressed?

Her feet were dragging as she climbed the wide staircase to her British Lit class. Steve was still passing out M&M's even though the voting was over. Ms. Oggle was passing out the *A Tale of Two Cities* papers. Victoria held her breath. She thought she'd get at least a B on it. But when she finally got hers it didn't have a grade on it. Victoria turned it over. On the back Ms. Oggle had written "See me." Her heart fell.

She looked over at Steve. He appeared to be reading his paper. She wanted to know what he'd gotten and why she hadn't gotten a grade at all.

After class everyone left but Victoria and Steve. They followed Ms. Oggle to her office on the third floor of the mansion. Victoria's heart was pounding so loud she was sure everyone on the whole campus could hear it. Ms. Oggle sat down behind her desk where she'd no doubt been intimidating students for the past fifty years.

"What's this about?" Steve asked, sitting down even though they hadn't been invited to sit down.

"You and Victoria have written very similar papers," Ms. Oggle said, peering at them with her gray eyes that matched her gray sweater that matched her gray tweed skirt. "I want to know why."

"I can explain," Steve said.

Stunned, Victoria looked at him. Was he going to confess he'd borrowed her paper and copied from it?

"Victoria's new here, so I gave her some advice about writing papers."

"Is that true?" Ms. Oggle fixed her gaze on Victoria.

"Well, yes, he told me to first say what I was going to say, then say it, then finish by saying what I'd already said. But I'd already written my paper."

"You said you were going to rewrite it after I helped you."

"Perhaps, Mr. Heller, you were too generous with your help. You may have helped her too much."

"But I didn't . . ." Victoria stammered. "He didn't . . ."

"These two papers are too similar," Ms. Oggle continued. "It cannot be just a coincidence. One of you has lifted material from the other. You know the punishment is the same for the person who gives help as the person who receives it."

"That doesn't seem fair," Steve said mildly.

"I will refer this matter to the Ethics Committee," Ms. Oggle said. "That's all."

thirty-three

It's immoral to steal, but you can take things.

—Golden Gate Fortune Cookies
(The cookie with the crunch)

Victoria felt like she was going to throw up. Her face was hot and her hands were cold as she gripped the polished wooden banister of the wide Manderley Hall staircase.

"Don't worry," Steve said. "The Ethics Committee is half students. Everyone cheats. They know that. What are they gonna do to us?"

"Us? Steve, you copied my paper!"

"Of course I didn't. I used some of the same ideas, just the ones we talked about in class, I'm guessing so did everyone else—guilt, shame, sacrifice. You know. That's not plagiarizing."

"Then why does Ms. Oggle think it is?" Victoria wondered how Steve knew what they'd discussed in class as he was hardly ever there.

"She's old, she doesn't know what's cheating these days and what's not. Probably never even submits a paper to turnitin.com to catch anyone. Half the kids are getting their papers off the Internet. I'd say we're in the minority, writing our own papers. We ought to get extra credit for that instead of being dragged in front of Ethics. Anyway, don't worry about it."

Why should she worry if he didn't? He was the one who'd copied her paper. Or had he? She had no way of really knowing since Ms. Oggle kept both papers.

"Can I see your paper?" she asked, stopping in front of the mansion's front portico.

"Haven't got a copy, sorry. But let's get together and do something soon, celebrate my victory. Just kidding. You might win. Have you seen the new Double O-Seven movie?"

What? Steve was asking her out on a date? At last. He wasn't too shy. He wasn't intimidated. He was doing the pursuing. He was *that* into her. For one crazy moment she forgot he'd just copied her paper and gotten them both into trouble. She forgot that he'd ruined her party. She forgot that she was not at all that into *him*. Then she realized the truth. He *had* copied her paper. Of course he had. That's why he was coming on to her.

"No, I . . ."

"I'll call you. And, Victoria—chill. I'm telling you everything's gonna be okay." He gave her one of his dazzling smiles and walked off toward the soccer field on the other side of campus.

Victoria walked slowly out to the parking lot. What had just happened and why? Had her dreams just come true or her worst nightmare? She was in serious trouble for doing something she hadn't done.

Gabe was leaning against her car, hands in his pockets. She was glad to see a friend. That's all he was, but that's just what she needed right now.

"You look like you got hit by a diesel truck. What happened, did you lose the election?" he asked.

"The election? I forgot all about it. You know that paper I wrote on *A Tale of Two Cities*? The teacher accused me of plagiarizing it from Steve Heller."

"The guy who ran against you for treasurer? The guy who . . . Why would you do that?"

"I didn't. He borrowed my paper the day class was canceled, so if anyone copied from anyone . . ."

"It was him," he said. "What a dick. And now you're in trouble?"

"I don't know. He says everyone cheats. Is that true?"

"At Castle it was. Here it's probably worse. More's at stake. Pushy parents expecting a lot. I should talk. My mom's the one who pushed me to get into Manderley."

"Like mine," she murmured. "She wants me to be like her."

"Mine's gotta be worse. She *doesn't* want me to be like her."

"I met her at Parent Night. I like her."

"I like her too. I'd like her a lot more if she'd tell me who my dad is."

There was a long silence. Victoria didn't want to go home and face an empty house. Remembering Cindy's sister's advice, she was afraid to ask Gabe to do anything, even go for a walk, stop for coffee. Sure, he was just a friend, but he was a guy and at certain times, like now, he did look a little like a tough, sexy spy with a cropped haircut. Which meant . . . She wasn't sure what it meant. She just didn't know how to handle guys at all. Especially when it turned out they weren't who you thought they were.

"Were you waiting for me?" she asked.

"Yeah, I have a flat tire. Wondered if I could catch a ride with you. I promise not to harass you about your car."

"That would be in bad taste," she said. "Considering."

"Not that I've changed my mind about emissions."

"I didn't think you had."

"You want to stop for coffee at Starbucks?" he asked.

"Sure," she said. Then she opened her trunk and he put his bike in after taking off the front wheel.

This was going to be awkward. Was he buying? Should she offer since she had plenty of money and he didn't? If he did pay, wasn't it just to thank her for giving him a ride? She'd only stopped at the coffee shop to get a latte to go, never to sit down with friends because it wasn't likely she'd have any to sit with. It was where the popular kids hung out after school. Maybe Gabe had gone there with his friends from his old school. If anyone saw them there, they wouldn't assume it was a date. So there was nothing to worry about. Besides, Gabe was the type who didn't care what people thought.

Today Cindy was there with Marco in a booth at the front near the window. Her eyes widened when she saw Victoria and Gabe walk in together.

"Did you win?" Cindy asked, scooting over to make room for them.

"I doubt it. They haven't finished counting the votes yet. It doesn't matter. In fact, I hope I didn't."

"Victoria, don't say that," Cindy said.

"Sorry," she said. "You guys worked so hard on my campaign." She changed the subject, but didn't mention her problem with her paper. Maybe if she didn't mention it, she could forget it for a while.

Other kids came by to say hello, or to ask about the election. Looking around she realized she'd turned a corner at Manderley. She had more than three friends. People who didn't know who she was before she ran for treasurer. Maybe it was good she ran after all.

They stood to leave when the manager came over and told Gabe it was good to see him and the coffee was on the house. He said they missed him, that no one made lattes as fast as he did, and asked when was he coming back to work.

Gabe said he was sorry, but he had too much homework. The manager told him he hadn't picked up his last paycheck. When Gabe opened the envelope his eyebrows shot up.

"So you worked there," she said after they'd left.

"Yeah. First time I've been back. Funny how different it feels on the other side of the counter."

Out on the sidewalk with Cindy and Marco, Victoria said, "I hope I don't sound like what's-her-name with the positive attitude . . ."

"Pollyanna?" Cindy asked.

"But I'm glad I ran for treasurer. It doesn't really matter if I win or not. I mean that. Campaigning was fun, thanks to you guys." She smiled at Gabe and Cindy. Then she turned away so they couldn't see her blink back a tear.

But Gabe saw.

"I like your attitude," he said.

"I like yours too."

"By the way," he said, putting a warm hand on her shoulder. "I've been thinking about the cheating thing. Steve says you copied his paper and you say he copied yours."

"I know I didn't copy his."

"I know that too. And I think I know how you can prove it."

thirty-four

A committee is a group of the unwilling picked from the unfit to do the unnecessary.

—Golden Gate Fortune Cookies
(Scrumptious!)

Steve was right. The Ethics Committee agreed that Steve and Victoria's papers were similar, but that's what happened when the whole class was supposed to be writing about themes in a classic book by Dickens. Besides, the kids on the committee blamed parents for lack of moral guidance.

"The problem is not us," a guy named Scott said. "It's adults and society—they aren't giving us any direction."

"What are we supposed to think when we see CEOs going to prison for lying to their investors?" a curly-haired girl asked indignantly. "I'll tell you what we think, we think cheating on tests is small potatoes."

"Right, the adult world is setting us a bad example," another guy added.

"Standing by your word, doing the right thing, these are things we haven't been taught," said another girl self-righteously.

They were so into their tirade, Victoria wondered if they even remembered who she was and why she was there. Or if she even needed to defend herself. She looked across the table at Steve, who looked relaxed and confident. He even winked at her. She knew he was thinking, *See, I told you so.*

She looked away. So he was right. They weren't really in trouble at all. She was relieved but still angry at him for taking advantage of her. Angry at herself for being so gullible. If the committee had decided against her, she could just picture Steve grinning, letting her take the fall and get suspended.

When the teachers, the adult committee members, spoke, they blamed everyone but themselves.

"Kids today think grades and test scores are more important than integrity," Mr. Jones, the physics teacher, said. Then he went on to suggest that maybe some parents hadn't supplied a "moral purpose in the home." Victoria thought he didn't know her parents. Jones looked at his watch, no doubt wishing this was over so he could get out of there.

"Honor is so not important. I mean it's like chivalry or the knights or whatever. No one believes in that crap anymore," said a guy with a headband.

"No one?"

Every head turned to look at the source of the comment. No one knew how long Mr. Kavanaugh, the headmaster, had been standing in the back of the room in his usual blazer with the American flag pin in his lapel. His bearing was just as military as when he'd commanded a whole battalion, and his eyes were scanning the room as if he were looking for snipers.

"Honor is what I have been entrusted to bring to this school," he said, crossing his arms over his chest. "Along with moral purpose. No one will stop me from my goal and no one will get away with plagiarism on my watch. No one. Is that understood?

The faculty members nodded vigorously, looking like there was nothing they wanted more than moral purpose and honor, when in fact what they wanted was to get out of there as fast as possible. The students mumbled various affirmative responses and reached for their backpacks.

"This committee is excused," Kavanaugh said. "In fact, this committee is abolished. From now on I am the Ethics Committee of one. Everyone out. Except for Ms. Lee and Mr. Heller."

There was a stampede for the door. Teachers shoving other

teachers, students desperately pushing their way through the open door and into the hall as if the flames of hell were licking at their heels.

When the room was empty except for the three of them, Victoria felt cold all over. She was alone with the two people she most wanted not to be alone with. She didn't want Steve to get away with cheating, but she didn't want the headmaster to take matters into his own hands either.

Who knew what he'd do with all that power he'd just assumed for himself? Who knew what punishment he'd mete out, and to whom? She could just imagine calling her parents to tell them she'd been suspended, kicked out for good . . . or . . . or . . .

Kavanaugh took a seat at the head of the table and removed two sets of papers from his briefcase. He leveled his hostile gaze first at Victoria, then at Steve.

"Ms. Oggle has provided me with copies of your papers," he said. "Before we get into the cheating allegations, I must say I am appalled at the number of spelling errors in your papers. I realize it is too much to ask a high school student to be proficient in spelling these days, but is it too much to ask you to run spell-check on your computer, assuming you do have a computer?"

"That's my fault, Mr. . . .Sir," Victoria stammered. "It's

not a good excuse, but I was in a rush. I know I'm not a good speller, but some of the errors are because I transferred from an international school in Hong Kong this year where we used the British spelling. Words like *defense* with a *c* instead of an *s*. Things like *rumour* and *colour* with a *u*. I plead guilty of misspelling, and I'm guilty of giving my paper to Steve to read before I turned it in, but I'm not guilty of plagiarism." Victoria was breathing hard. She couldn't believe she'd actually said all that without a pause. And without notes.

"So you blame your former school for your spelling deficiency?" he snapped.

"No, I only meant . . ."

"I see what she's doing," Steve said, leaning across the table, a knowing smile on his face.

"Quiet," Kavanaugh said so sharply Steve's smile disappeared and he slid back down in his chair as if he'd been struck on the head. His eyes met Victoria's and she could feel waves of fury coming across the table in her direction. Steve hated her. He'd expected her to take the blame for him.

There was a long, uncomfortable silence. She knew what Steve thought of her, but what about Kavanaugh? He kept turning the papers in front of him over and over and making marks in the margins with his pen.

"And you, Heller," he said, raising his eyes to look at Steve.

"What is your excuse for these same spelling errors? Were you also at an international school last year?"

"No," Steve said. "But wait, I didn't cheat. I can prove it. I'll take a lie detector test. I'll do anything you say."

"That won't be necessary," Kavanaugh said. "It's obvious to me what has happened here. I don't need a committee or a polygraph test to see what is in front of my eyes. Ms. Lee, you are excused, with this caveat: Do not ever lend your paper to a friend to read again before turning it in. Is that clear?"

"Yes, sir. Thank you."

"I will deal with Mr. Heller. Suffice it to say, he will not be assuming the office of class treasurer. That office will now go to you by default."

Victoria nodded. Her knees were weak but she stood and made it to the door. As she passed Steve, he muttered, "Bitch." And as she closed the door behind her she heard Steve shout at the headmaster, "You can't prove anything. My father is a lawyer and he . . ." Then she stumbled down the stairs and across the campus.

She passed the stone senior bench where the popular upperclassmen hung out, she passed the nerds playing chess under a tree, but she really didn't see anyone at all. Her feet felt like lead and her heart was thumping erratically.

She sat in her car with her forehead pressed against the

steering wheel while she tried to make sense of what had happened, first the committee, then the headmaster. If only she'd gone straight home she would have missed Steve. Instead he stood outside her car, banging on the glass with his knuckles until she lowered the window a few inches.

His face, which she'd once thought was so gorgeously all-American she could picture it on a Wheaties box, was almost purple with rage.

"You slut," he said, wrapping his fingers around the top of the window. "You know what you did to me, don't you?"

"Me? I didn't do anything to you."

"Oh, no? British spelling. International school. Couldn't you keep your mouth shut? No, you had to rat on me."

"I didn't. I just said . . ."

"I know what you said. You had it all planned, didn't you? Words like *defence, colour* and *rumour.* You're just as much to blame for this as I am. You gave me your paper. What did you think I was gonna do with it?"

"You're right, Steve. I was stupid. I should have known. But I didn't. I didn't know you were a cheat."

"And you know what else?"

"You mean that I'm the treasurer and you're not? Is it really all that important?"

"I don't give a rat's ass about being treasurer. The headmaster is putting the plagiarism thing in my file, which will show up in my college recommendations. My parents won't stand for that. My father's going to be royally pissed and he'll fight this. This isn't the end of this. He'll be so fried at you and at the headmaster. This is your fault. All yours!"

Victoria hesitated only for a second before she jabbed her finger on the window control. The motor whirred and the window closed and stalled as it squeezed Steve's fingers.

He yelped.

She lowered the window just enough for him to pull his fingers out. "Bye, Steve," she said.

thirty-five

If winning isn't everything, why do they keep score?

—Golden Gate Fortune Cookies
(A cookie too good to be true)

When the election results were posted the next day and Victoria saw she was listed as the winner, she didn't know what to say or who to tell that she'd really won by default. But if she told the truth, it would be telling on Steve, so maybe it was best to let everyone think she'd really won fairly.

It wasn't what she wanted. What good would it do her to have class treasurer on her resume when she went to design school anyway?

And she was going to design school. She'd even told her parents who were so thrilled to hear about her being treasurer that it didn't register that Victoria was not going to follow in their footsteps. It would register eventually. And she'd have to deal with them later.

Gabe was waiting for her at her car. So far he was the only one she'd told the truth to, since it was his idea to use the spelling errors to prove her innocence. She hadn't even told Cindy and Maggie the truth. They were so excited she hadn't had the heart to do it. Not yet.

Gabe's bike was propped against the trunk of her car. If this was getting to be a habit, she was starting to like it.

"Race you home," he said.

"You're on," she said.

"Is there a prize for the winner?" he asked.

"Better be. Because I'm going to win. You're not dealing with a nobody here. You're challenging the junior class treasurer." She took a deep breath. "If by some lucky chance you win, what do you want?"

"Have you seen the new kung fu movie?"

"Why, are you asking me on a date?" she asked. Fat chance. He wasn't the dating type. She'd like to be, but she wasn't either.

"Yeah, I am. Maybe we could have dinner first. Have you been to the Left Bank?"

"The French restaurant in Menlo Green? No."

"Neither have I. Want to go with me?"

"You're asking me to dinner and a movie?" she said. She must have spaced out for a minute.

"Why not?"

She wanted to say, *Because we're opposites. Because I'm rich and you're poor. Because you can't afford it. Because . . . because . . . you don't even like me. Or do you?*

"What's wrong?" he said. "I thought you said you liked European food and action movies."

"I do but . . . do you?"

"There's a first time for everything."

"That must have been some check."

"It was. Counting tips and everything."

"You don't have to spend it all on one date."

"I won't. I'm saving some for the second one."

She took a deep breath. "Where I come from, the girl pays for the second date," she said.

"Yeah?"

"Another thing, how are we getting there? On your bike?"

"I'll borrow my mom's car. It's a hybrid."

"Like me."

"A lot like you. Cool looking, small, efficient, handles well and keeps up with everyone else on the road. And, oh yeah, like the Lexus, you're a luxury package."

The look in his eyes made her heart trip in her chest. She

shivered, but it was a good kind of shiver. So it was true. When men are into you, they do all the work. They say nice things to you. They challenge you to drive faster than they bike. They ask you out on a real date.

Of course it helps if you slow your car to twenty-five miles per hour just to be sure you lose. It was just as important to be a good winner as it was to be a good loser. This week she'd had a chance to be both. Too bad Steve didn't understand that. Maybe after he got back from his one-week suspension he'd have a better attitude. Or not.

Gabe won the race and was waiting for her in the driveway with a grin on his face.

"I would have won but there was traffic," she said.

"Yeah, sure."

She switched the subject to chemistry and asked him what would happen when the DNA results came back from the lab.

"What if there are no matches for you?" she asked.

"There won't be," he said soberly. "My dad is not a teacher. My dad died a long time ago."

"What? How do you know?"

"My mom finally told me when I explained about my experiment with the DNA tests. I think she felt bad I was going to all that trouble to find out. My dad was married and had a family. That's why the big hush-hush. But he left a trust fund for my education. That's how I can go to Manderley and college after that."

"How do you feel about it?" Victoria asked, studying his face. He looked all right, but with Gabe she never really knew. He was good at covering up his feelings.

"I'm okay with it. I'm sorry I never knew him. But guess what? He was a designer. Had a studio in Palo Alto where they designed all kinds of stuff for Silicon Valley."

"An artist. Oh, Gabe." Her eyes filled with tears. Tears for the guy who never knew his father and tears for the father who never knew what a great, talented son he had.

"Got a minute? I want to show you something," he said. He took her hand and led her into the garage. He turned on the light. There on the wall was a dazzling burst of colors and shapes.

"Oh, my God, you did it. It's beautiful." She walked up close to look at the brush strokes.

"Careful, don't get too close. I have some touch-up to do," he said.

"Your father would be so proud of you."

"Think so?"

"Sure of it."

He had a faraway look in his eyes. Maybe imagining showing his father the mural. Then his gaze came back to her.

"Now it's your turn to do your thing," he said. "Your dye experiment thing."

"I've got all the chemicals to mix it up. You sure you want to help me?"

"We're partners. We work together. You heard what the man said. It's the scientific way. You know, there's another experiment we can try at home he didn't mention." Gabe's eyes gleamed, and he gave her the sexiest smile she'd ever seen on him . . . or on anybody.

"What's that?" she asked breathlessly. But she already knew. She barely had time to put her hands on his shoulders and close her eyes, before he kissed her.

It was chemistry. Most experiments don't set off bangs, flashes and explosions. But this one did. After that she forgot about technique. All she had to do was throw her arms around his neck and hold on. Because when you're dealing with chemistry, you'd better be prepared for the earth to shake as the atoms bond and the elements react. In the lab or at home.

Remember Rule Number One: To prove your experiment, it has to be repeatable. You have to get the same earth-shaking results under all different conditions, like day and night, rain or sun, kitchen, garage or your four-poster bed.

* * *

That night Victoria took out her *A Tale of Two Cities* paper and rewrote the last line. She deleted "It was the worst of times," and printed out in bold letters "IT WAS THE BEST OF TIMES," and stuck it to her mirror where she could see it. Because it was.

And now a special preview of the next book in the BFF series . . .

The Guy Next Door
A BFF Novel

Coming from Berkley JAM
May 2008!!!

one

It was a dark and stormy night when Maggie and her mother left their McMansion in Monte Vista and moved to a small rental house in Carlmont. Six months later, the weather had improved, but not much else. Her parents' divorce was under way, and the house where she grew up was for sale.

"Listen to this," her mother said, rattling the pages of the Silicon Valley newspaper's real estate section. " 'Classic Spanish villa in prime Monte Vista, eat-in kitchen with granite counters.' " She looked up, her eyes blazing. "*My* granite counters. *My* eat-in kitchen."

Maggie grabbed her backpack and looked over her mother's

shoulder. " 'Private tree-studded setting,' " she read. A pang of nostalgia hit her between the ribs. Tree studded was right. Tree studded with *tree house.* Or had her father taken down the tree house after she'd left along with the volleyball net and the tetherball pole?

It didn't matter. She was way too old for backyard sports or the tree house where she'd once played with her best friend Ethan Andrews. She picked up her duffel bag full of her fencing gear. That was her sport now. Fencing was fast, athletic and challenging. Just what she needed to take her mind off other problems. "Gotta go. I'll be late for school."

Her mother said nothing, not even good-bye. Her face was blocked by the newspaper, but Maggie knew how she'd look. The way she'd looked for the past year, brow furrowed, eyebrows knitted together, her mouth in an angry frown.

Maggie could have reminded her that the sooner the house was sold, the sooner there'd be a settlement, but her mother was sunk too far in depression to be cheered by anything Maggie would say.

It was a relief to get to school. Away from her mother's despair that hung over the house like a blanket of San Francisco fog. At least it wasn't an apartment. Maggie shuddered to think how that would affect her mother who'd once had a gardener, a cleaning service and a personal trainer all come to her house in the private, tree-studded setting.

While everything else in her life had changed, Maggie was still at Manderley Prep, the most expensive, the most exclusive high school in the Bay Area, maybe the whole state of California. Let her father take up with a new girlfriend, let him complain about the way she and her mother spent his money. As long as he kept paying her $28,000 tuition, she wouldn't say a word against him.

If she were completely honest she'd admit that one of the big reasons she loved the school was not the spacious campus, the small classes, the 10-to-1 student-faculty ratio or even the snob appeal of rubbing elbows with the spawn of Silicon Valley's famous movers and shakers. It was the opportunity to see Ethan every day.

This was her lucky day. There he was, tossing a Frisbee across the lawn to one of his friends. So casual, so incredibly effortless. She didn't even have to wait until sixth period Chemistry class or Mixed Chorus to get her Ethan fix for the day. Not that they ever spoke or hung out anymore. Except for one night when he'd come by the ice-cream store where she worked; he never even looked in her direction. Not in the classroom or the cafeteria or out here on the grass. That hurt.

She didn't expect him to be her BFF the way he was when they were kids. Or take pictures for the school paper of her fencing in competitions the way he did other girls in more popular sports. Just a simple "hi" would be nice considering . . .

She set her bag on the ground and watched him from under a blue Jacaranda tree Gertrude Manderley herself had imported from South America over one hundred years ago. Maggie hoped to blend in to the scenery and not appear awe struck at the sight of Ethan's tall, rangy body and broad shoulders.

Some guys go through an awkward stage, either skinny and clumsy or short and pudgy. Ethan never had. He was a cute little kid who'd grown up to be impossibly good-looking with dark curly hair and strong features.

"Enjoying the view?" Her friend Victoria Lee had come up behind her. As usual she was dressed in the latest skinny jeans, leather sandals showing off manicured toenails and a fitted jacket right out of *Teen Vogue* she'd probably made herself.

"Who's the hottie over there?"

"Ethan Andrews. An old friend, that's all."

"Maggie, you're holding out on us. Old, how old?"

"Used to live next door to us. Or rather we used to live next door to him. Our parents were best friends and so were we. Not anymore."

"Oh, because of the divorce?"

"Because we grew up. Do you think guys and girls can really be friends after a certain age?" *Please say no. Tell me it's not because he doesn't like me. It's just the way it is. Guys turn their backs on the past while girls hang on.*

Victoria shook her head. "I don't know. My old friends are far away in Hong Kong. I live next door to Gabe. If I didn't I might never have gotten to know him."

Gabe was Victoria's housekeeper's son who lived above the garage on the Lee's estate. No one thought they'd ever be a couple. But they were.

"When I first met him I didn't want to be his friend and he sure didn't want to be mine."

"And now you're madly, truly, deeply," Maggie said with a sigh.

If Victoria wasn't such a good friend, Maggie would have hated her for her exotic half-Asian looks, her clothes, her money and her boyfriend, but she didn't. Victoria was modest and generous to a fault and a good friend just when Maggie needed friends the most.

Ever since the divorce, her old friends had drifted away just like her mother's had. It wasn't as if divorce was a dirty word around there or something to be ashamed of. Loads of kids lived half the time with one parent and half with the other.

But for her, it seemed like she was the one who was divorced—from her house, her friends and her former generous weekly allowance.

Victoria grinned at Maggie, showing perfect teeth. If only Maggie had her braces off she might grin too. But she didn't. She had a mouth full of metal she was stuck with for at least another eight months, according to the orthodontist, which seemed like an eternity. Unless of course she replaced them with the costly invisible kind. The braces weren't the only reason Maggie didn't smile these days. There was the constant tension between her parents, her mother's depression and always the nonstop worries about money.

"It's your turn," Victoria said. "Cindy's got Marco and I've got Gabe. If you want Ethan, you need to go after him. Does he have a girlfriend? Because if so, Cindy and I will get rid of her for you." Her two new friends amazed her. Both of them vigorously pursued their goals. And it paid off. If only she had their tenacity and their confidence to get what she wanted.

The idea of perfectly groomed fashionista Victoria snatching away a girlfriend from Ethan just because Maggie wanted him for herself was so touching and so completely ludicrous Maggie had to smile in spite of herself and expose her braces.

Curious, Maggie asked, "How would you get rid of her?"

"Oh, I don't know, tie her to a block of cement and dump her in the Bay."

Maggie gasped. Knowing how Victoria had the guts to live on her own while her parents lived in Hong Kong, she wouldn't put anything past her.

"Who're you dumping in the Bay?" Tall, red-haired Cindy Ellis appeared at that moment, a well-worn clarinet case under one arm.

"See the Greek god over there?" Victoria asked. "Maggie likes him, I mean she really likes him and if he's got a girlfriend, we've got to get rid of her."

"Count me in," Cindy said. "Spring fling is coming up. Let's all go together."

"Look," Maggie said with a hint of desperation. "I appreciate your advice and all, but there's no frigging way Ethan will ask me to the dance. Besides, I'm scheduled to work at the Super Scoop every Friday and Saturday night." If she didn't have the job, she'd have to invent one to have an excuse, besides being unpopular, for not going out on the weekends.

"Then ask *him*, and take one night off. Come on, you deserve it."

"Oh, right. How would that work? I call and ask him to the dance and he says, 'Maggie who? The girl who wrestled all the boys to the ground in kindergarten? The girl who showed no mercy in backyard volleyball games?' See, I used to be a tomboy once," she explained. "And he would never think of me as a date for a dance or anything."

Her friends had obviously forgotten what life was like before they had a boyfriend. Forgotten that sinking feeling in the pit of the stomach when *he* was in your class, the nervous tick in the eyelid when you ran into *him* unexpectedly on campus, the shaking hand when punching in a certain phone number then hanging up when you got *his* voice mail.

"Cindy, I remember when you had a crush on Marco. Don't tell me you would have asked him to a dance then?"

"That's different," Cindy said. "I didn't spend my childhood playing with Marco in my backyard. I didn't know him. I was new here and so was he. He probably would have passed out from shock if I'd asked him to a dance. But it's perfectly okay for you to do it. In fact, he could be sitting around wondering why doesn't anyone ask me to the dance?"

"She's right," Victoria said. "Sure, he might be surprised that you're asking him to the dance. But it could be a good surprise. Ever think of that?"

Maggie shook her head. They just didn't understand. If Ethan wanted to go out with her, he would have asked her. It was that simple.

"Oh," Victoria said, her face lighting up, "there's Gabe. I

need to talk to him. See you guys later." With a wave to her friends, Victoria cut across the lawn to catch her boyfriend.

"Later," Cindy said, heading off to leave her clarinet in her locker before her first class.

Maggie went straight to the Manderley Hall, the centerpiece of the school where founder Gertrude Manderley had once lived and hosted the rich and famous at her salons, and even the poor especially if they were outrageously bohemian and artsy enough to catch Gertrude's attention.

Being childless, Gertrude had left her house to be turned into a school, and a scholarship fund for financially challenged smart kids like Cindy and Gabe. There were stories of how much Gertrude *hated* boring people almost as much as she hated boring trees like oak and redwood, which she had removed and replaced with exotic imports. Among other famous quotes, she'd supposedly said, "If you haven't got anything nice to say about anyone, come and sit next to me."

Maggie hurried down the stairs to the basement, the site of Gertrude's private bowling alley which was now used by the fencing club. There was just enough time to drop off her equipment and make it to first-period English.

The light from the overhead fluorescent bulb was so dim Maggie could barely read the sign on the door with her glasses.

"Fencing Club canceled until further notice." Signed Newton Kavanaugh, Ret. Col., Headmaster.

She dropped her duffel bag and reread the note. What did it mean? Fencing was her sport. Instead of spreading herself thin playing soccer in the fall, tennis in spring and basketball in the winter, she was concentrating on fencing year-round.

They couldn't take it away from her. She loved everything about it, the lunges, the escape moves and the strategy. It was like chess with a sword. The hits were mere touches and scored electronically, but it felt real. More real than anything else she did these days. And it was a way to get noticed by college recruiters.

She heard footsteps. Someone else was coming. Maybe Greg Townsend, who taught history and coached fencing in his spare time. Now she'd get an answer.

It wasn't Greg, it was Ethan. Her knees buckled. She licked her dry lips, snatched her glasses off and stuck them in her pocket. What on earth was he doing here?

"This the fencing room?" he asked. "Oh, Maggie, it's you." He sounded disappointed, just as he would if she had the nerve to call and ask him to the dance. *Oh, Maggie, it's you, he'd say.*

"Hi, Ethan." Why did her voice sound so high and tinny? "It *was* the fencing room. I don't know what's going on." She tried the door and it swung open. The large, cavernous room was dark and damp. Just what you'd expect from a basement. Since there are no basements in the typical California house, no one expected anything from Gertrude's former bowling alley. There was a huge mirror on one wall. A must in fencing for determining what's wrong with your position. Looking down at your feet was a no-no. Just the mirror, that was all. No mats, no weapons or any other sign there was once a fencing club here.

"The lacrosse coach sent me to sign up for fencing."

"You mean Greg? Why?"

"He said it would be good for footwork and balance and hand control. My dodging and protection could use some work too if I'm going to play lacrosse for one of the big schools."

"Like your father." Maggie remembered Ethan's father played football for UC Berkeley. Loyal alums, his parents hosted a tailgate party at their house before every game. Naturally, her family was always invited too. Not anymore. Maybe her father still saw the Andrews socially, but they'd dropped her mother like she had a communicable disease.

"Like my father? I'll never be like my father," he said. "I hope. You fence?"

"Yeah, I do. I mean I did. If there's no after-school club, I don't fence." Sure, there were private clubs, that's how Maggie had learned to fence, but those days of country clubs and private lessons of any kind were gone for good.

"Bet you're good at it. You were always a good athlete."

If only he remembered something else about her. But that was too much to ask.

"So what's the big deal with fencing?" he asked. "How come you do it and not . . . I don't know . . . swimming or tennis? You really like swinging from chandeliers and jumping off balconies?" He grinned. Even in the dim light she saw his teeth were perfectly straight and dazzling white. It was something she couldn't help noticing. Everybody had a big bright smile. Everybody but her. If you went to Manderley, you had enough money for orthodontics and by the time you were a junior, they were gone.

If Maggie didn't have those Ugly Betty braces, she would have smiled back. "It's not like that. It's more like two people doing a dance. I don't know why I can't dance, but I can fence. It's really fun if you do it right. For me it's a challenge and it's a good workout too. You know the fights in *Stars Wars* with the lightsabers? That's what fencing is supposed to look like."

"Knowing you, you're not afraid of getting hurt," he said, looking at her with narrowed eyes. He must be remembering she was game to jump out of the tree house or sommersault off the board at his pool. She wasn't even afraid of spiders in the garage. No wonder he'd never think of her as a girlfriend. She'd never been a girly-girl and it was too late to start now.

"Not with the right equipment," she said. "Fencing's actually safer than football or lacrosse. You just have to project a calm, confident image. That's a big part of fencing. Same with all sports, I guess."

He nodded. "Look tough, act tough. Stare down your opponent."

"Right. Even in fencing when you have a mask in front of your eyes." She pointed to her duffel bag. "Glove, jacket, plastron, chest protector, mask . . . That's the kind of stuff you need."

"Where do I get them?"

"I can give you the catalog. But wait, there may not be any fencing at Manderley."

"Well, I gotta find a private coach then. Who's yours?"

He thought she still lived a privileged life of personal trainers and coaches. He had no idea what was going on in her life. Once she moved away, she was out of sight and out of mind. No, it was way before she moved, even before junior high. All of a sudden, for him, she didn't exist.

"I haven't got a coach now, but I did. I'll get you his name and number."

"Thanks," he said.

Maggie closed the door and they walked up the steps together in awkward silence. She had a dozen questions, but none she had the nerve to ask.

Thinks like, *"Do you have a girlfriend now? Is it your blond-bimbo chemistry partner or one of those girls in chorus who're always falling all over you?"*

"Do you remember when we used to run naked through the sprinklers on your back lawn?"

"What did you get on your last chemistry test?"

"How did you do on your PSATs?"

"Why don't your parents ever call my mother?"

Finally she came up with something less personal. "Are you still writing articles for *Manderley in Motion*?" He'd once told her he wanted to be a photo journalist like his uncle who was a foreign correspondent. But that was years ago.

"I had an article in last week's issue," he said. "I guess it made a big impression on you."

"Oh, sorry I didn't see it." Good one, Maggie. How had she missed it? "What was it about?"

"The new SATs. I can't tell you what a black hole that fell into. You're not the only one who didn't see it. I really wanted to write about how the school's changed this year. Closing certain clubs, like the Gay and Lesbian Alliance, canceling cheerleading. But I needed an interview with Kavanaugh, to get his side of the story. I had an appointment, but he canceled on me. Said he had nothing to say. So I've got one more nail in the coffin. 'If fencing goes, what's left?' "

"I don't think many people know there is a fencing club. Or care."

"That's the point. Things are disappearing and no one knows or cares. Maybe they should."

"Yeah." She couldn't believe it. She was having a real conversation with Ethan. He was confiding in her. It was almost like old times. There were so many things she wanted to talk about. Questions she was dying to ask. Had he seen her father? Had he complained about her spending too much money? Was her father seeing someone else? Had he remodeled? Torn down her tree house? Ripped up the vegetable garden and planted roses? But she didn't know where to start.

"Saw a for-sale sign on your house," he said.

"Oh, uh, that's right."

"Seems weird without you there. Just your dad and . . ."

She froze. "And who?"

He didn't answer. He just said, "See you, Maggie," and joined the throngs of kids on their way to first period.

Wait, she wanted to say. *What about the exposé you're writing? What about fencing? When will I give you the coach's number?*

Berkley Jam delivers the drama

Not Anything (Available February 2008)
by Carmen Rodrigues

After her mother's death, Susie Shannon closed herself off from the world—until Danny Diaz helps her open her heart again.

Violet by Design (Available March 2008)
by Melissa Walker

The lure of international travel draws Violet back into the glamorous world of modeling, and all the drama it brings with it.

Twisted Sisters (Available April 2008)
by Stephanie Hale

Aspen Brooks thought that college would be a dream—but between investigating a student's disappearance and fending off her boyfriend's roommate, who insists he's in love with her, it's turning out to be one big nightmare.

Go to penguin.com to order!